PRIVATE DANCER

BERKLEY HEAT TITLES BY SHERI WHITEFEATHER

Private Dancer

Wedding Favors
(with Nikita Black and Allyson James)

Masquerade

PRIVATE DANCER

SHERI WHITEFEATHER

HEAT
New York

THE BERKLEY PUBLISHING GROUP
Published by the Penguin Group
Penguin Group (USA) Inc.
375 Hudson Street, New York, New York 10014, USA
Penguin Group (Canada), 90 Eglinton Avenue East, Suite 700, Toronto, Ontario M4P 2Y3, Canada
(a division of Pearson Penguin Canada Inc.)
Penguin Books Ltd., 80 Strand, London WC2R 0RL, England
Penguin Group Ireland, 25 St. Stephen's Green, Dublin 2, Ireland (a division of Penguin Books Ltd.)
Penguin Group (Australia), 250 Camberwell Road, Camberwell, Victoria 3124, Australia
(a division of Pearson Australia Group Pty. Ltd.)
Penguin Books India Pvt. Ltd., 11 Community Centre, Panchsheel Park, New Delhi—110 017, India
Penguin Group (NZ), 67 Apollo Drive, Rosedale, North Shore 0632, New Zealand
(a division of Pearson New Zealand Ltd.)
Penguin Books (South Africa) (Pty.) Ltd., 24 Sturdee Avenue, Rosebank, Johannesburg 2196,
South Africa

Penguin Books Ltd., Registered Offices: 80 Strand, London WC2R 0RL, England

This book is an original publication of The Berkley Publishing Group.

This is a work of fiction. Names, characters, places, and incidents either are the product of the author's imagination or are used fictitiously, and any resemblance to actual persons, living or dead, business establishments, events, or locales is entirely coincidental. The publisher does not have any control over and does not assume any responsibility for author or third-party websites or their content.

PRINTING HISTORY
Heat trade paperback edition / August 2010

Library of Congress Cataloging-in-Publication Data

Whitefeather, Sheri.
    Private dancer / Sheri Whitefeather.—Heat trade pbk. ed.
       p. cm.
    ISBN 978-0-425-23457-0 (trade pbk.)
    1. Stripteasers—Fiction. I. Title.
PS3623.H5798P75 2010
813'.6—dc22   2010006714

PRINTED IN THE UNITED STATES OF AMERICA

10 9 8 7 6 5 4 3 2 1

To Starr, Shilo and Shannon—
the exotic dancers I once knew

PROLOGUE

AN INDEPENDENT NATION IN THE MEDITERRANEAN REGION
LATE EIGHTEENTH CENTURY

I always knew that Prince David Abir Rou Veli, the heir to the Neylan Empire, was going to be my husband. I, Princess Camille Renard, had been promised to him since I was a child. As a little girl, I used to imagine him as a kind-hearted boy who would grow into a romantically noble man.

But my dreams about him were nonsense.

Wildly handsome, Prince David was also spoiled and barbaric, and I dreaded the thought of becoming his bride.

Nonetheless, we were about to be wed.

At this very moment, I waited in the primary courtyard of the palace for my bridegroom to appear in a royal procession. Already I could see a throng of torches headed my way, held aloft in the night sky. Beside me were my female attendants.

Earlier, I had been groomed in an ancient method called smoothing, where my body hair had been removed with a syrupy paste and strips of muslin, leaving my pubis shamefully bare.

Afterward, they had bathed me in milk, a tradition of purification, followed by scented oils. They had also arranged my long dark hair in an elaborate style, covering their handiwork with a delicate veil that also shrouded my face.

My dress was a sparkling caftan made of the finest white silk and adorned with the most precious of jewels.

I glanced down at my hands. They had been decorated in a ritualistic blessing, where a renowned artist had painted an intricate design, using a paste made from a dried plant. This was meant to ward off evil spirits, bring luck, and increase fertility. But much to my dismay, my soon-to-be husband's name was also hidden within the complex pattern.

Beneath my veil, I tempered my expression. Prince David's parents, the sultan and his European-born queen, would be arriving in the royal procession, several paces behind their son.

Although the sultan took deep pride in his customs, the queen influenced the culture, as well. Some of her practices had been absorbed into society, creating mixed traditions.

Like the queen, I, too, hailed from a small European country, and my marriage had been arranged to protect alliances and retain royal bloodlines.

I understood this. I accepted it. As a child, I had been taught to speak the Neylanic language, preparing for this day.

But the one thing I could not fathom was the sultan's harem. Although he was only permitted one wife, he kept a bevy of beautiful women at his disposal, and the queen accepted this without reservation.

Me? I did not want to be married to a man who openly called upon other women. But Prince David had a harem, too. I, of course, had been aware of this all along, but I had requested that once we were wed, he would respect my wishes and disband his harem. But he had told me, in no uncertain terms, that he intended to keep his women.

Heaven, how I hated him.

As the procession got closer, as the torches drew nearer, I detested the notion of our wedding night. I suspected that after he dutifully bedded me, he would send me back to my chambers and summon one of his other women.

A harem beauty who would curl up beside him while I soothed the ache from our coupling and battled the urge to cry myself to sleep.

CHAPTER ONE

Beverly Gilbert added a little more blush to her luminously bronzed skin, then sat back to evaluate her reflection in the mirror.

Her wedding garb consisted of skimpy lingerie and a short, flouncing white dress, where her surgically enhanced breasts spilled out over the top.

For the final touch, she clipped a rhinestone headpiece into her long, thickly waved blond hair, but she didn't cover her face with the attached veil. She still had a bit of time to spare.

"Hey, Malibu!"

Beverly turned to the sound of her stage name. The high-pitched call had come from Delilah, another dancer at The Dusky Doll. Delilah, a chatty brunette, was dressed like a

Roman goddess, and beneath her micro-mini toga was a G-string decorated with gold grape leaves.

As always, Delilah was peering out from behind the dressing room curtain, checking out the clientele.

Beverly preferred not to think about the crowd, not until it was her turn to dance and the opening song she'd requested was played.

Delilah closed the curtain and made a face. "Don't freak out, okay?"

"What are you talking about? Why would I?"

"I think I saw your husband at the tip rail."

Beverly started. "You mean my *ex*-husband?" Jay Novak, she thought, the man she'd divorced more than two years ago. "It can't be him. He would never come here." They'd met at the club, but they'd split up over it, too.

"Maybe it's just some guy who looks like him."

Yes, that had to be it. About a month ago, a man bearing a striking resemblance to Jay had sat at the tip rail with a gorgeous brunette by his side. They'd made Beverly so nervous she'd almost messed up her routine. But they'd left right after she'd danced, and she hadn't seen them since.

"Do you want me to double check?" Delilah asked, offering to peer out from behind the curtain again. "Or you could take a quick peek yourself."

"No. It's fine." What reason would Jay have for invading her turf? "I'm on soon anyway."

"Then you'll know for sure."

"I already know it isn't him."

"He's hot, whoever he is."

"*Delilah.*"

"Sorry." The Roman goddess adjusted a bobby pin in her loosely styled upswept hair. "I'm just making conversation."

Beverly wanted to tell her to go make it somewhere else, but Delilah wasn't the enemy.

So who was? Jay?

Between the whirlwind courtship and hasty vows, they hadn't even made it past the first year. But that didn't mean that she hadn't loved him.

Clearing him from her mind, Beverly returned her attention to the mirror and covered her face with the veil.

Once she was ready, she waited by the curtain to make her appearance. The tall, tanned, green-eyed siren.

The naughty California bride.

As the intro to Billy Idol's "White Wedding" began to play—the song she'd picked—the DJ introduced "Malibu."

Whoosh.

Beverly dashed through the red velvet curtain and onto the stage, scanning the tip-rail patrons. The hard-edged music pounded through her soul, but that was nothing compared to what seeing him did to her heart.

There he was. Not someone who resembled Jay. The real thing.

Gorgeous as ever, he sat parallel to the pole, at the center of the horseshoe-curved stage, which had been his favorite spot when he'd courted her.

His short, light brown hair was stylishly messy, and although he surveyed her every move, he showed no emotion. His face was a blank canvas, shrouded in male mystery.

Torn between strutting straight up to him and getting the hell out of Dodge, she headed for the pole and swung her long, lethal body around it.

If Beverly was the ultimate California girl, then Jay was the supreme California guy. As a model/actor, he had grown up in the Valley, surfing, skateboarding and snowboarding. To support his craft and his sports, he moonlighted as a fusion-style cook.

A tasty man who made tasty food. A man who'd wanted her to quit dancing once she'd become his wife.

Well, screw him, she thought. Between Jay and her family, no one supported her choices.

She climbed the pole, knowing he was watching. The club was filled with people, but he was the only one on her radar. He looked like a mirage through her filmy veil. A long, tall, forbidden drink of water.

"White Wedding" was all of four minutes and ten seconds, but already it seemed like the longest song in history.

By the time her pole work was done and she was lifting her veil, a poignant line in the second verse blasted through the speakers.

I've been away for so long.

As Beverly got down on her hands and knees and crawled across the stage, collecting ones and fives in the process, she was inexplicably drawn to her ex.

When she came to him, she stood up and peeled off her dress, turning around to flash him her G-stringed rear.

Was that her way of telling him to kiss her ass? She honestly didn't know because she spun back around and unhooked her bustier, baring her full Ds.

Taking it to the next level, she licked the tips of her fingers and wet her nipples, smiling like the naughty bride she was supposed to be. If she hadn't been such a professional, her face would've cracked. Flirting with him, even in a theatrical way, was painful.

He didn't return the smile. But she had him just the same. He leaned forward in his chair, and she knew she'd just given him the makings of a hard-on. He couldn't take his eyes off her. He seemed afraid to blink, as if he would miss something, even though it was a routine he'd seen a zillion times.

Beverly stayed close enough to tease him, to make his cock stiff, but not close enough to let him breathe her in.

Then he held up a neatly folded bill, offering her a tip.

Damn. Now she had to get closer.

Oh, what the hell, she thought, and sat down on the edge of the stage. Perched directly in front of him, she opened her legs while she moved to the music, giving him a deliberate peep show.

Not that he could see anything but the crotch of her G-string, but it was the illusion that counted. He, of all people, knew what she looked like beneath the white swatch of lace.

She leaned forward so he could put the bill in the top of her garter belt, and as he made the transfer, his fingers skimmed her leg.

Instantly chilled and immediately aroused, Beverly struggled with the urge to remove her G-string. But she couldn't. The Dusky Doll was a topless club, not a full nude.

Jay looked into her eyes, and she fought another aroused chill. He still hadn't smiled, but the energy between them was palpable. Some of the other club goers were tossing money at her, enjoying what she doing to Jay. She even shoved her foot against his chest, thrusting a six-inch heel at him.

Her message was clear: Fuck me if you dare. But it was just part of the game, she thought. The act.

Wasn't it?

Her heart was pounding so hard she could've sworn that Billy Idol was kicking the inside of her chest.

Thud . . . thud . . . thud . . .

Still seated in front of Jay, she imbedded her heel a little deeper, and he stared at her with blatant lust.

Thank goodness the song was nearly over.

She stood up to complete her routine, turning away from

her ex and winking at a group of men on the other side of the rail. They were young and silly and rowdy, bachelor-party guys.

Finally, she was done. She gathered her belongings and collected her tips without glancing back at Jay.

Once she was safe and secure in the backstage dressing room, she lifted the bill he'd tucked into her garter belt.

In the background she could hear the next song, "Money for Nothing," chosen by Starla, a dancer who masqueraded as an eighties rocker.

Money for nothing and chicks for free.

Beverly begged to differ with the lyrics, but the song wasn't about her dance-for-dollars world.

It wasn't about her painful marriage, either.

She glanced at her left hand where the diamond Jay had given her used to be. She still had it, tucked away in a jewelry drawer at home. They'd both paid a price for walking down the aisle. Nothing between them had come for free.

But she'd moved on. Not only did she work here, but she taught pole, lap and striptease lessons to regular women.

Women who wanted to get into shape. Women who wanted to learn how to entice their men. Women who simply needed to feel good about themselves.

A sensuous and empowering form of fitness. What could be more rewarding than that?

Regardless, Beverly needed to focus on the here and now.

She put her wedding attire back on and headed for the main floor.

Would Jay still be there, waiting to talk to her, to buy her a drink, to solicit her for a memory-lane lap dance?

Lord, she hoped not. But she knew enough about men to be prepared for anything.

Sure enough, he was there. He'd taken a table in the corner, but she noticed him right off.

From across the room, their gazes met and held.

Before anyone, including the bachelor-party boys, approached her, she wound her way around the club, striding over to Jay's table.

"What are you doing here?" she asked, taking what she hoped was a position of power.

He didn't seem impressed, but he was good at positions of power, too.

"Some friends thought I should revisit my old haunt," he said.

"Your old haunt or your old wife?"

He finally flashed the smile he'd been withholding. "She still looks pretty young to me."

"Smart aleck."

He had one of those casual grins that made women melt. A dangerous side of his power. She imagined kissing him—an extremely stupid urge for a highly intelligent girl.

He gestured for her to sit. "Come on, I'll buy you a drink."

Later he would ask for a private dance. She could see the intention in his eyes.

Although she knew it would behoove her to walk away, she accepted the chair he offered.

When the cocktail waitress came by, Beverly ordered a cherry Coke. Jay was already nursing a beer.

"So, who are the friends you mentioned?" she asked.

"Amber and Luke. You haven't met them, but they were here once."

Her senses went on alert. The beautiful couple who'd watched her dance? "The girl who looks like a fashion model and the guy who looks like you?"

"Yes. That's them. We were having a ménage at the time. But they're together now. Just the two of them. They even got engaged."

She considered snarling at him, but she clamped her jaw shut. The ménage part stuck in her craw.

Finally she asked, "Since when were you into three-somes?"

"I'm not. I mean, I was then, but I'm not now. It was Amber's idea. She wanted both of us."

Right, blame it on the girl. "But she's marrying him?"

"She loves him, and he loves her. I could tell it was happening from the beginning. But they were in denial." Jay pulled on his beer. "Before they admitted how they felt about each other, we had this phony honeymoon night."

"The three of you?"

He nodded. "It was a masquerade. Luke and I were made up to look exactly alike. We wore tuxedos and black masks, and she was in a wedding gown."

Beverly didn't want to hear about his kinky adventures, but sat there and listened anyway.

"We even took mock vows. I guess we all had our reasons for doing it."

She was tempted to ask him what his reason had been, but there was a part of her, the wife she'd once been, who couldn't bear to know.

Her Coke arrived, and he put it on his tab.

"I live with them," he said. "I'm their roommate. But eventually I plan to move out."

She sipped her drink, wishing she'd gotten something harder. The sweet cherry flavor seemed too innocent, too sock hop for the atmosphere.

Before things turned quiet, he asked, "So, what have you been doing?" He gestured to her outfit. "Besides flashing your panties and making your ex-husband hard?"

She played coy. "You got hard?"

"You know damn well I did."

"Then you shouldn't have come here."

"They convinced me I should."

They, she thought. Amber and Luke. "Well, they were wrong. You shouldn't have."

"Yeah, but it's too late. I'm already here."

And he'd already gotten hard, which meant that he wouldn't be leaving anytime soon, and certainly not without the lap dance he craved.

"If you really want to know what I've been doing," she said, putting off the dance for a little longer, "I've been getting regressed."

He gave her a blank stare.

She explained. "Hypnosis that takes you into your past lives."

"You're kidding?" He flashed his girl-melting smile. "Who did you used to be?"

"A European princess who married a Middle Eastern prince."

His eyebrows shot up. "That sounds like a hypnosis-induced fantasy to me."

"I should've known better than to tell you."

"Come on, Bev. You have to admit, it's a little weird, like a fairy tale or something."

"If I was going to concoct a past life for myself, I wouldn't have created a husband who has a harem."

"Oh, wow. He had other women. That sucks."

Beverly wanted to fling her syrupy drink at him. He was grinning like a sexy loon. "Screw you, Jay."

"Sorry." His grin faded. "I just don't know if I believe in that stuff."

"Believe in what? Harems?" She went deliberately prim. "That seems right up your alley. You and your three-somes."

"I was talking about past lives."

She knew exactly what he was talking about. "Princess Camille hated him."

"Hated who? Her husband?" Jay shook his head. "So much for my timing."

"This doesn't have anything to do with you."

"Maybe you divorced me as payback for him."

"I didn't even know about him when I divorced you."

"Not in your conscious mind. But maybe in your heart, it affected how you felt about me."

For a guy who wasn't sure if he believed in past life regression, he was quick to shift the blame.

"I divorced *you* because of *you*," she said, making her point clear and wishing her heart hadn't been mentioned.

He defended himself. "What kind of husband can stand his wife dancing for other men?"

She went smug. "Oh, I don't know. The kind who knew that she was a dancer when he married her?"

"Fine. Dance for me now." He pointed to the second story. "Up there. On a private couch."

The couches weren't as secluded as they seemed. Shadow-shrouded bouncers kept the activity in check. But it was as close to private as it got.

Beverly had no business dancing for someone she'd once loved, but she couldn't seem to stop herself.

They stood up, and she reached for Jay's hand.

It was customary for the dancer to take the client's hand and lead the way to the couches. Nonetheless, the connection of their clasped fingers sent shock waves up her arm.

Along with the recurring urge to kiss him.

CHAPTER TWO

Would he kiss me? Would that arouse his lust and make his duty more bearable?

And what about my clothes? Would he take the liberty of removing my wedding dress or would he expect me to discard the sparkling caftan myself?

The lavish ceremony and grand celebration was over. He was my husband now, and I was being escorted to his bedchamber. My apartment was in the women's quarters, near his harem. But unlike the harem, there was no courtyard that separated us. This was the privilege of a wife, I had been told, to be able to visit her husband in such a convenient manner.

Of course, that did not matter to me. I would lie with him,

*as often as necessary, but only for the sake of an heir. Once my
womb swelled from his seed, I would keep my distance.*

*During our vows, he had played his royal part, seemingly
respectful of his bride, but I had caught the aloofness in his
eyes. Later, at the celebration, he had continued to look right
through me.*

So here I was—the invisible wife, nervous beyond compare.

*Baki, the slave who led me to my husband's apartment, was
the chief custodian of the prince's harem. Baki was a big man
with a robust face and a heavy beard. He was also a eunuch.*

*But knowing that he had been castrated did little to ease my
discomfort. It only made me more aware that my husband's
genitals were fully intact.*

*Baki paused at an ornately carved door affixed with cop-
per bolts. He handed me a dressing gown that had been designed as lounging attire, should I choose to wear it after the
deflowering.*

*With his head bowed, he said, "His Royal Highness re-
quested that you enter on your own."*

*I wanted to beg the slave to stay, to not abandon me this
way. But I dismissed Baki instead, and he took his leave.*

*As he walked away, I watched him. He headed toward the
courtyard of the harem, then disappeared from view.*

*I had yet to see the prince's harem, and this was not a good
time to envision it, much less the women who resided there.
But my mind kept straying in that direction.*

How many women did he have? Did they kneel naked at his feet and wait for his instruction? Did he bestow gifts upon them for their services? Did he punish them if they displeased him?

One thing I knew for certain was that they were not permitted to bear his offspring and measures were taken to inhibit conception. From what I understood, this was not common among other harems. Most were filled with women and children. But in Neylan, only a wife could provide a royal heir— hence my purpose.

I gazed at the gilded door in front of me. I could not remain on this side of it forever. Sooner or later, I would have to summon the courage to open it.

Maybe I could feign a sudden illness. Maybe I could buy myself time. For what? Prolonging the inevitable?

No, I thought. I was a new bride, and this was the night my marriage was meant to be consummated.

I turned the door handle and entered my husband's bedchamber. Like everything at the palace, it was saturated with luxurious silks and woven damasks. Amid the opulence were cool marble floors, colorful rugs and painted archways.

Brass lanterns burned softly, and a long elegant runway led to a platform-raised, canopy-draped bed.

I noticed him instantly, as he was there, waiting for me. He looked arrogantly relaxed, leaning against an array of vibrant cushions.

He, too, still wore his wedding attire, a jeweled tunic and loose-fitting pants. He had, however, removed his coiled headdress, just as I had removed my veil. Although our hair was nearly the same shade, his complexion was much darker.

I moved forward, slowly, taking the runway. Finally, I stopped and placed my dressing gown on a bench at the foot of his bed.

David, I thought, analyzing his name in my mind. The translation was Daoud, pronounced Da-ood. But his mother had insisted upon David. Either way, it meant beloved.

In the silence, he tilted his head, and I studied his features.

His catlike eyes were flecked with gold and deeply set below naturally winged brows. His nose carried fine, straight lines, and his nostrils flared, albeit slightly. His beard was trimmed close to his jaw, enhancing the handsome angles of his face. From what I had heard, he did not use a barber; the women from his harem groomed him.

I frowned, and he gestured to a platter of candied fruits beside the bed.

To sweeten me up?

"No, thank you," I said in his native tongue.

"You barely ate at the celebration," he responded in the same language.

I had been too nervous to fill my stomach then, just as I was too anxiety-ridden to pummel it with treats now.

"In my homeland, women eat sparingly," I said. And wear petticoats and corsets, I thought.

"We are not in your homeland" was his cool remark.

"I am aware of where we are," I retorted. How could I not be aware? I was naked beneath my straight-lined dress, my body smoothed of its hair.

He lifted those winged brows at me, letting me know that he found my outburst unbecoming.

But I did not care what he thought.

He patted the space next to him. "Join me, Camille."

In spite of the impatience in his voice, my name on his lips gave me a shiver. Somewhere in the recesses of my mind, my childhood dreams threatened to surface.

Willing those romantic notions away—for what good would they do?—I approached him, then removed my sandals and climbed into his canopied bed.

His feet were already bare. He had rings on his toes, peculiar adornments for a man, yet common to this region.

He moved closer to me, so close I could smell the sandalwood on his skin.

"Are you afraid?" he asked.

I was more than afraid. I was terrified. But I said, "Should I be?"

He gave no response. Instead, his gaze swept the length of me, the gold in his eyes rivaling the amber light that bathed the room.

Struggling to keep my wits, I noticed a pot of tea on the bedside table closest to him. The candied fruit was on the table nearest to me.

"I will take some tea," I said, hoping the hot beverage would help settle my nerves.

"Shall I summon a kitchen servant to pour it for you?" he asked. All he had to do was pull one of the color-coded cords beside the bed to provide whatever type of service he required. I, too, had similar cords in my apartment.

I chose to help myself. At this point, I thought, the presence of a servant, however brief that might be, would only increase the tension.

Unfortunately I had to lean past him to reach the pot and china cups. While I was in this prone position, I could feel him watching me.

Finally, I managed to pour a solitary cup and settle back down.

He frowned, then reached across my body to grab a handful of dates.

As I sipped my tea, he popped the dried fruit into his mouth. One by one, he chewed, spitting the seeds into a container.

Once the dates were gone, he removed his tunic and tossed the garment aside.

He looked incredibly virile without his shirt. A dusting of hair whirled coarsely around his flat brown nipples. The tightness of his stomach drew my nervous attention, too. Be-

low his navel was a line of hair that quite obviously led to his pubis.

"Why are we playing this game?" he asked suddenly.

"What game?"

He took my teacup and placed it on the table. "You pretending that you are not afraid this first time and me pretending that I do not desire you."

My heart fluttered. Childhood dreams. Sweet and buoyant. "You desire me?"

He grasped a lock of my hair, threading it through his fingers. "From the moment I first saw you."

I clung to a ray of hope. "Do you desire me enough to disband your harem?" Had he finally come to see the error of his ways?

"No," he said flatly, crushing my fluttering heart. "One wife could never replace an entire harem." He lowered his hands, preparing to disrobe me. "No matter how beautiful she is."

~

Damn, but she was beautiful, Jay thought. His wife.

Ex-wife, he corrected. Beverly didn't belong to him anymore. But then, she never really had. He'd been forced to share her with other men. Not literally, of course. But metaphorically, that was what being married to an exotic dancer had felt like.

They ascended the stairs, and he squinted into the dimly lit atmosphere. The second floor was where the magic happened.

Private dances. Wild fantasies.

Honestly, what the hell was he doing here? He knew better than put himself through this.

Still, he sat on a crushed-velvet couch and said, "Make it dirty," challenging her to a client-dancer duel.

She hesitated, but only for a moment.

Then, as if to say, "You're on," she placed her hands on his thighs and thrust his legs open. His pulse went straight to his cock, and he cursed Luke and Amber for talking him into reevaluating his feelings for his ex.

She stood between his legs and loosened the front of her dress, allowing a bit more of her bountiful cleavage to show. The only area of the club she was permitted to be topless was on stage, so she was giving him the next best thing.

Also, according to house rules, Jay was restricted from touching her, and she was supposed to remain within six inches from him. It was called air dancing, a form of a lap dance that didn't actually involve climbing into the customer's lap.

Yet there was something about the way she was sizing him up, something about the way she seemed to be considering her options.

Would she break the rules? She never had before. Beverly was a good little stripper who played by the local jurisdiction book. But he figured she was due. What could be sweeter than dry humping your ex, then telling him to hit the road?

She glanced at the big, burly bouncer in the corner. Was she signaling for him to turn a blind eye? Jay didn't recognize the guy. In fact, none of the bouncers looked familiar. But two years had passed since Jay had graced The Dusky Doll, and strip clubs had notoriously high turnover rates. Not only did security change, dancers often came and went, too.

But not Beverly. Not the woman he'd foolishly married. She was still doing her white-lace and hot-promises routine.

She quit making nice with the bouncer and shifted her attention back to Jay.

"Almost ready," she said.

Yeah, almost, he thought.

She nudged his legs open a little wider. She was killing time, waiting for the song that played to end and for the next one to begin. The timing had to be just right. When you paid for a dance, you got a full song.

She leaned closer, and Jay felt like a man who was about to drown in his own blood.

He wished he'd never met her, let alone put himself in the position of being her ex. Luke and Amber thought he was still in love with her. But Jay couldn't say one way or the other. All he knew was that he wanted her back in his bed.

Pow!

The next song started—George Michael's "I Want Your Sex." Christ, he thought, could it get any worse?

Beverly mastered the raunchy rhythm and rolled her perfect body toward his.

He gripped the couch to keep from grabbing her. He remembered how it felt to be inside her, to push hard and deep.

He wanted her sex, all right. He wanted her big fake tits and warm wet pussy. He wanted to ride her like an oil-slicked seesaw. But he wanted to hold her afterward, too. The way a man held his wife.

Shit.

She got close enough to make him suffer, to tempt him with the concept of breaking the rules.

Would she or wouldn't she?

Just do it, he thought. *Please, do it.*

She did. She climbed in his lap. Jay held his breath. Waiting, waiting . . .

Yes, there. Right *there*. She rubbed against his fly, back and forth, giving him the erection of a lifetime.

He tipped his head back against the cushion and looked up at her. Her long blond hair fell forward, cloaking the sides of her face: stunning green eyes, a bit of sparkle on her cheekbones. And her lips, those luscious lips. He imagined stealing a kiss.

Would she taste the same?

Mint and sugar with a dash of cream. The first time

they'd kissed had been on their first date, and he couldn't get enough.

And now here he was, getting a post-divorce dance.

As she ground against his lap, her phony little wedding dress flared, hiding the naughtiness of the act.

Secret seduction. Broken rules.

She even reached under her dress and touched herself. Or he assumed that was what she was doing. He couldn't see exactly where her hand was, but he got the gist of it.

She was probably faking it, making it appear as if she was rubbing her clit while she humped him. But damn, it was effective.

He prayed that he didn't lose control. That he didn't come in his pants.

"Feels good," she said.

"Yeah" was about all he could manage.

Good, good, good. Bad, bad, bad. She knew how to drive him to sexual distraction. She knew how his mind worked. She knew what turned him on. His former bride. The hot blonde who climbed poles.

Jay's pole ached like a mother.

Beverly removed her hand from under her dress and ran a quick finger across his lips.

He nearly salivated. *Had* she been touching herself? He didn't know. He couldn't tell.

"Do that again," he said.

She shook her head. "One time is all you get."

Not fair, he thought. But he'd brought this upon himself.

She continued to dance; she continued to grind. Then she went primal and got down on her knees.

Lord Almighty.

She made an erotic motion with her hands, right against his fly, as if she were stroking his cock and putting it in her mouth.

Every cell in Jay's body burned from the desperate want of her. What she was doing was hot and trashy and much too public. The dimness of the club was a façade, and he was her willing pawn.

God, he hated himself for that.

Torn between fighting for his dumb-ass dignity and praying for relief, he waited for her next move.

When she climbed back onto his lap, they both went a little mad. She humped him so hard and fast, he groaned and grabbed her waist. He lifted his hips, too, pushing back against the pressure.

Fucking without really fucking.

The song ended, and they stared at each other. He couldn't fathom a more awkward moment. He forced out his breath, and she sucked in hers.

Stripper's remorse?

Now that it was over, she seemed uncomfortable about how far she'd gone. Regardless, she was still straddling his lap.

Refusing to let it end on a graceless note, he leaned forward and kissed her. Softly, slowly. The kind of kiss that said he missed her.

He felt her tremble beneath his touch, but she kissed him back.

Almost as if she were still his wife.

~

I wished I was not his wife. But wishing would not change the course of reality.

As David removed my caftan, I thought, once again, about how he refused to give up his harem.

Hurt and anger swirled like poison in my veins, and I stared at him with defiance.

He reacted by raising those annoying brows. Then, as if to challenge me, he cupped my breasts.

"Pretty," he said. "Very pretty."

I assumed that he meant my nipples. They had been rouged by my bridal attendants and were as pink as wild geraniums.

He rubbed them, and they grew into hard little buds. A smile snaked across his lips, heightening my indignation. The sensation he incited was soft and butterfly sweet, but I with-held the feeling, refusing to give him the satisfaction of reacting favorably to his touch. He would get nothing from the princess he married.

While I remained stiff and passionless, he continued to explore me. He lowered his hands, skimming my waist and hip bones.

He had an artistic way about him, like a sculptor or a painter. But still, I refused to let him affect me. When he circled my navel, I turned my head away.

I had been told that some of his harem girls wore jewels in their navels and danced seductively for him.

They were his slaves, yet I envied the carnal power they possessed.

He cupped my mound, and I held my breath. As he slid a finger halfway inside, I winced from the invasion. Or was it humiliation? The knowledge that I, his wife, the girl who had dreamed of him, was second best?

"Look at me," he said.

With distain, I turned back to face him.

"You are insolent," he said.

"Would you prefer that I were meek?"

"I would prefer that you try to enjoy this." He pushed his finger deeper, then moved it in and out, creating a copulating rhythm.

But once again, I refused to yield to him, to show even the slightest stirring.

With a frustrated breath, he removed his finger and said, "I could use my mouth on you."

The thought of him lapping between my legs made me

strangely weak, but I remained combative, narrowing my eyes. "I do not see how that will make a difference."

"I have a skilled tongue."

"According to whom? Your other women?" I paused for effect. "Is that what they have been trained to say?"

He hastened a retort. "If you were not the sacred vessel for my child, I would toss you into the sea."

I did not snap back at him. I simply lay there, intent on making his effort to impregnate me as unpleasant as possible.

He shoved down his pants and freed his penis. Much to my surprise, he was fully erect. Was that my power? Making him hard, even in the name of anger?

As a woman, my triumph was clear, but as a wife, it felt hollow.

I stared at the ceiling as he mounted me. His body was strong and solid against mine, his skin warm to the touch, but I did my best to ignore the masculine weight of him.

He did not attempt to kiss me, for which I was grateful. I feared that the sugared dates he had eaten would have made him taste lustfully sweet, worsening my lonely plight.

As he nudged my legs apart, I prayed that his seed spilled swiftly.

He pushed into me, and I clawed the bed cover with henna-painted hands. Pain seized my loins, fueling a caustic ache. He thrust deeper, and my discomfort heightened. He was all the way inside.

I sensed that he was looking at me, frowning as he shattered my maidenhead. But I could not be certain. I was studying the mosaic pattern on the ceiling.

From there, he moved at a median pace, neither harsh nor gentle. Without my participation, he was simply doing what had to be done. I suppose I should have appreciated his restraint. He could have given me a deliberate pounding and intensified my pain.

Then again, maybe that would have been easier—all the more reason to hate him.

I was not his first virgin, nor, I suspected, would I be his last. In the slave trade, untouched women were sought after. In the wife trade, too. I had saved myself for this heart-wrenching moment.

Finally the discomfort in my loins began to subside. But I was still encumbered. The sting in my chest remained.

As he increased the tempo and worked toward his release, I wondered what I would see if I looked at him.

Would his face be an indiscernible mask? Or would there be animalistic pleasure in his catlike eyes—a natural reaction he could not control?

In spite of my curiosity, I continued to avert my gaze from his.

Still, I was burdened with the feel of him, the scent of him, the sound of him. I was even burdened with his name.

I thought about how it was hidden in the pattern on my

hands. Eventually, the stain would disappear. But that would not release me from him.

He groaned deep in his throat and arched his quaking body. His seed spilled into me, bathing my inner walls with milky warmth.

My heart skipped a pulsating beat, and he pulled away from me, leaving a musky scent dangling between us.

He got out of bed, and I finally looked his way, catching a disturbing glimpse of his nakedness. His penis remained slightly erect, the color ruddier than before. From my maiden's blood, I thought.

He tossed my dressing gown at me. "Put this on, and I will summon Baki to take you back to your apartment."

I quickly covered myself. Already the wetness between my thighs was leaking.

David pulled the green cord beside the bed, and in the silence that followed, he headed toward his private bath.

But before he reached the sunken tub, he turned back around.

"Oh, and tell Baki to send in a housekeeper to change the sheets." After a slight pause, he added, "Also tell him to send in one of my girls to bathe me."

My eyes burned with the threat of tears, but I frostily asked, "Any preference of who she is?"

"No," he responded, his voice just as chilly. "Any of them will be a welcome change over you."

CHAPTER THREE

Beverly knew better than to let this happen, but Jay's kiss tasted so good, so familiar. Snuggled on his lap and feeling nostalgically romantic, she rubbed softly against him.

He was gentle, too. He slid his hands down the curve of her spine, skimming the lace on her dress. She'd never intended to be a bride, not on stage and not in real life. She'd become a bride at The Dusky Doll because at the time she'd gotten hired, the former bride had just quit and they needed a replacement.

As for becoming Jay's wife, she'd simply fallen in love. Simply? Nothing was simple when it came to Jay.

He intensified the warmth, tilting his head at a deeper angle and playing sweet games with her tongue. He had this way of ravishing a woman when her guard was down. Or maybe it was just the way he affected Beverly, the way he made her feel.

Funny, she thought, how dreamily they were behaving, there at the club, with music pounding and other dancers doing their tip-me thing. It wasn't something she would have envisioned, and certainly not now that they were divorced.

Divorced.

The word bounced like a springboard in her head, and she pulled her mouth away, leaving him staring at her.

He blinked, clearly fighting to come to his senses. But his senses must have remained skewed, because in typical male fashion, he asked, "What's wrong?"

Beverly gave him a "get real" look.

Reality registered in his eyes, but he ignored it and went male again, motioning to the tight space between them. "There's nothing wrong with this. We're just making ourselves feel good."

Wonderfully good, she thought. Wildly good. But that wasn't the point. Anyone with half a brain cell knew that ex-spouses shouldn't mess with the past.

She climbed off his lap and smoothed her dress. She adjusted her cleavage to a slightly less in-your-face level, too. Not that it made much of a difference. She still looked like a fantasy bride.

She struggled for a solution. "I'll forget that you were here if you will."

"It won't be easy."

All she wanted was for this moment to end. By now the club was closing in on her. "Yes, it will."

Jay didn't seem convinced. Truthfully, neither was she. But she was doing her damnedest to tell herself that when she went home tonight, she wouldn't obsess about him.

He scooted to the edge of the couch, his body language tense. Hers was, too. She stood there in her ridiculously high heels, teetering on her feet.

"Have you been with anyone?" he asked.

She started. "What?"

"Have you slept with anyone since you left me?"

Out of fear, out of loneliness, out of everything that hurt inside, Beverly went on the attack. "That's none of your business."

He didn't take offense to her tone. Instead, he quietly said, "I haven't been with anyone except Amber. But Luke was there, too."

The threesome, she thought. She hadn't expected that to be his only encounter. Should she go ahead and tell him about her love life? Or lack thereof?

She opted for the truth. "I've been celibate, but I didn't want to rush into a rebound. Besides, most of the men I meet are customers, and dating them isn't a good idea."

"You dated me."

"Yes, and look where it got us."

"Missing each other?" He stood up, putting them face-to-face.

She considered backing away, but she figured it was foolish to make a nervous fuss.

"We should have an affair," he said.

Okay, now it was time for a nervous fuss. She went ahead and took some steps backward, but it didn't help because he moved forward. In the process, she pinned herself against a garishly papered wall.

"An affair?" She was trying not to envision it, trying not to give it credence. "Why? Because you think I need sex?"

"I think you need it with me, and I know I need it with you."

When he reached out to grasp a lock of her hair, she thought about the way David had touched Camille's hair on their wedding night, just seconds before he'd shattered her heart.

"Go home, Jay."

"I don't want to."

"I could have you kicked out."

"Yes, you could." He released her hair and backed away, holding his hands out in front of him, as if to say that he didn't have any tricks up his sleeve. "But I'm not going to push you that far."

"Then say good-bye and get out of here."

His voice went soft. "Bye, Bev."

She crossed her arms, wrapping herself in a troubled hug, and watched him descend the stairs.

Tall and proud, he disappeared without glancing back.

~

On the morning after my wedding night, I felt like a prisoner in my husband's palace.

Soon after I awakened, two young women aided in my toilet. In my country, ladies of the bedchamber would have performed those duties. Here, anyone who attended a royal was simply called a personal servant.

Of course, some servants were slaves, like the harem girls and the eunuchs who guarded them. But that was something I did not want to think about on this homesick morning.

By the time my toilet was complete, I was attired in a multicolored caftan with my hair flowing down my back. While in the women's quarters, veils were not required.

After my breakfast arrived, the personal servants left me alone in my apartment, creating a deeper sense of loneliness.

I tasted the food, a hearty porridge, seasoned with unfamiliar spices and accompanied by goat cheese, flatbread and ruby-seeded fruit.

It was unusually good, but nonetheless, I could not seem to finish it. As was the case yesterday, my appetite waned.

Rather than battle with my meal, I went outside and sat on a bench in my private garden, a place where the ground was covered in tiles and divided into large sectors.

Trees, flowers and shrubs grew in geometric planters, some of which were shaped like stars.

In Neylan, gardens were celebrated in poetry and considered locations of love.

Was it any wonder that I was alone in such a beautiful setting? If my childhood dreams had come to fruition, I would be sharing this moment with David.

My unbeloved.

Naturally I was curious as to what type of woman had stayed the night with him. Was she Asian or African or possibly European, like myself? Or was she a girl from this region?

Struggling to clear my mind, I breathed in the aroma of fruit trees and flowers. But it did not help. My thoughts remained cluttered.

Finally I decided that it was time to see David's harem. No one would think it odd, considering the customs here. The queen herself often visited the sultan's harem, befriending his other women and spending her afternoons with them.

I had no intention of behaving as graciously as the queen. I simply needed to sate my curiosity. After that, I would keep to myself.

Determined to make an impression, I returned to my bedchamber and adorned my caftan with a wedding gift from David's parents—a ruby necklace that glittered like fire. If I had been given a ceremonial crown, I would have worn that, too, but crowns were not customary here.

Either way, the harem girls would know who I was. No doubt I had been described to them. No doubt they had been gathering information about the princess their master had married.

I left my apartment and glanced toward the hallway that led to David's bedchamber. Was he still there? Lounging with last night's lover?

No, I thought. By now, he was probably at the stables, dressed in his riding breeches and cantering one of his prized horses.

I continued in the direction of his harem, and after entering the courtyard, I came to a large domed structure with pillared archways.

I did not enter the building, but I assumed that it contained the women's rooms. I also noticed a smaller building. Comparable in construction, but not nearly as fancy, I surmised it was the eunuch's quarters.

As I moved toward the center of the courtyard, I encountered a garden, similar to mine, with flowers, shrubs and nut-bearing trees.

Beyond the greenery, I heard the distinctive chatter of female voices, along with splashes of water.

I stalled to take a steadying breath.

From there, I followed the sound into a den of debauchery, my sight filled with naked women.

Some washed their bared bodies in a large luxurious bath while others played in an equally large rinsing pool, dousing each other like naughty mermaids. Others leaned backward, pointing their breasts to the sky.

A fair-skinned redhead lounging off to the side with her limbs comfortably spread, glanced up and gasped. "The princess is here!"

Although she spoke in the Neylanic tongue, I recognized her accent as British. I made eye contact with her, and she leaped up from her leisure to honor me.

Her body swayed as she made her way toward me. Her nipples were pierced and her navel was jeweled, both of which made her look wildly exotic.

Immediately, the others joined her, and there were scores of naked women, maybe twenty or so, bowing at my feet and dripping with water. They varied in height and coloring, but all of them were lusciously curved and delicately smoothed, the slits in their pubic regions glistening.

Soon the harem was in commotion, and another group of beauties appeared from the other direction, where the buildings were located.

Attired in a variety of filmy clothing, they, too, got on their knees. I estimated about thirty women in total.

Baki showed up, moving swiftly, as well.

"Your Highness." He also bowed. "May I offer you a chair? A cup of juice?"

Nervous as I was, I maintained my decorum.

"I am here to inquire about the girl who shared the prince's bed last night," I responded, royal as could be. "Who did you choose for him?" I looked past him and said, "Which one of you was it?"

"It was me," a sultry voice in the crowd answered.

I glanced around to see who she was and noticed a striking brunette.

I motioned for everyone to stand, and they collectively came to their feet.

I peered at the brunette, studying her deep complexion and lush brown hair. She was, by far, one of the most beautiful girls there. Although the kohl around her eyes was smeared, probably from the night before, it did not detract from her appearance. If anything, it enhanced her stunning qualities.

She wore a hazy blouse and a sheer skirt. She was naked underneath, and I could see the sleek, shadowy lines of her body.

"Did you serve him well?" I asked

"I bathed him," she responded. "And after he was clean, I gave him oral pleasure."

"Did you sleep in his arms?"

"Yes."

She spoke softly, almost lovingly, and her response made my heart hurt. At that horrific moment, I wanted to cry.

"What is your name?" I asked.

"*Sarila.*"

I turned to Baki. "Why did you choose her?"

The eunuch said, "I think she resembles you, Your Highness. And to me, that seemed fitting for the prince's wedding night."

"I tried to be a good substitute," Sarila remarked.

Humiliation curled in my belly. They all knew that I had not satisfied my husband.

To save face, I said, "I am still learning about the ways of lovemaking."

Sarila glanced around the harem. "We know everything there is to know. But we have been taught what to do."

I appreciated her candor, but I was still aching inside. I waved my hands, allowing the girls to return to their activities. They flurried and flitted, like butterflies cast out of a net.

Sarila began to strip, readying herself for a bath. The pierced and jeweled redhead came over to her, and they sank into the water together, then giggled and splashed like schoolgirls.

I watched them, wishing my life was that simple.

～

At 1:00 A.M., Beverly got off work and went home to her apartment. She entered through the front door, hit the main light switch and looked around.

It wasn't the same place she'd shared with Jay, but she had the same furniture. When they'd gotten together, they'd bought all new stuff, and when they'd split, he'd told her to keep it.

The décor was modern with black leather sofas and glass tables. She'd been considering adding Middle Eastern and Moorish accents like Persian rugs, mosaic-framed mirrors and henna lamps.

She couldn't help being attracted to things that reminded her of Neylan. Of course, now that she'd seen Jay, she was even more empathic of Camille and her struggle with David. It didn't get much worse than aching over your husband. Then again, Beverly thought, aching over your ex wasn't a picnic, either.

Maybe she should've taken him up on his offer; maybe she should've agreed to an affair.

And maybe she should just pull out the vibrator in her nightstand drawer and be done with it.

With a sigh, she went into her room, removed her clothes and tossed them in the hamper.

Would the vibrator help? Or was this one of those times when making mechanical love to herself would only heighten her loneliness?

Damn Jay, anyway.

She opened the drawer and removed the device, a classic style that women had been using since the fifties. Or at least progressive women, she supposed.

Beverly turned it on and watched it hum, but she didn't roll it across her breasts or down her stomach, the way she usually did to get in the mood. She just sat on the edge of the bed, staring at the stupid thing.

Once again, she cursed Jay. But she was at fault, too. She was the one who'd grinded against him tonight, who'd rubbed his cock, who'd broken the rules.

Flustered, she turned off the battery-operated toy, put it back in the drawer and glanced at the landline phone.

Should she call him?

She picked up the receiver and listened to the dial tone. He was probably asleep by now. Then again, he could be out on the town, distracting himself with the L.A. nightlife. He could've even gone to another strip club.

God, she hated feeling like this. No guy was worth it. Still, she dialed his cell phone, chiding herself for remembering the number so easily.

It rang and rang, and just when she expected his voice mail to come on, he answered.

"Hello?" He sounded groggy.

She pictured him in a darkened bedroom, where the call had jarred him awake. At least he wasn't at a club.

"Hi," she responded. "It's me. Bev," she added, in case he was too discombobulated to make the mental connection.

"Hey." He came huskily to life. "What are you doing?"

She fought a sexy shiver and looked at the drawer where her vibrator had been put to rest. "Nothing."

He went silent for a moment, then asked, "Are you going to invite me over?"

She wanted to say yes, but suddenly she couldn't bring herself to admit her weakness. "Maybe we should just talk on the phone."

"What good will that do?"

Her mind raced for an answer. Clearly she was confused. Horny and scared. "We could say things to each other."

"You mean dirty things?"

"It's just an idea." A chicken's way out, she thought.

He turned silent again. Either that or the call had been dropped.

She waited a beat. "Jay? Are you there?"

"Yes, I'm here. But I'm not playing around on the phone with you. If you want to get nasty, it's going to be in person."

Her pulse zoomed straight to her pussy, and she squeezed her thighs together. "How nasty?"

"Anything you want."

Heaven help her, but she wanted everything. She wanted a sexual smorgasbord. "I shouldn't be doing this."

"Does that mean I can come over?"

"Yes." This time the word came out before she could stop it.

She gave him her address, and he said, "Be good until I get there."

She glanced at her clenched thighs. "Should I get dressed?"

"Why? Are you naked?"

"Yes."

"Hell, no, you shouldn't get dressed. You should answer the door just like that."

She didn't listen. After they hung up, she put on a luxurious silk robe she'd bought just that week—a colorful garment that was sleek and soft and fit for a harem girl. Or a princess, she thought, at the height of a husbandly affair.

Much too nervous, Beverly waited. Finally, after twenty excruciating minutes went by, a knock sounded.

She opened it, and there stood Jay, shrouded in the dark of night. She'd forgotten to turn on the porch light. He came inside, and they stared at each other.

He looked handsomely disheveled, a sign that he'd climbed hastily out of bed, grabbed the first T-shirt and jeans he could find, then jumped in the car. He'd probably driven like a madman, too, and in flip-flops, no less.

"You're not naked," he said.

She tried to explain the robe. "I wore this because it's new, and it makes me feel like Camille."

He frowned. "The princess?"

She nodded, wishing her feelings made more sense. As it were, she was torn between herself and the woman she used to be.

"What was her husband's name?" Jay asked.

"David." But because it sounded too simple, she added, "His Royal Highness Prince David Abir Rou Veli."

He traced the collar of her robe, and Beverly's heart pounded. He was moments away from baring her body. She could feel the anxiousness in his touch.

His hands slid down the fabric. "Why did she hate him?"

Beverly responded on Camille's behalf. "It was more of a love-hate thing."

"Like the fine line between the two?"

"Yes."

"So, in actuality, she loved him?"

"Yes," she said again, but since this was a terrible time to dwell on love, she didn't expound.

Nor did Jay seem to want her to. He dropped the conversation, too.

But he didn't lose sight of his agenda. He tore open her robe, tossed it on the floor and swooped down to kiss her.

In the midst of pawing each other, of roaming their hands in teenage-type fury, they stumbled in the wrong direction. Instead of going to her room and falling into bed, they landed in the kitchen, with him pressing her against a cabinet.

His fly bulged, and the denim grazed her mound, but she didn't care. She pulled him even closer, and they kissed again.

When they came up for air, Beverly went for it.

Beyond foreplay, she dug her fingers into his T-shirt and yanked it over his head. She battled with his zipper, too. At the moment, all she wanted was him inside her.

When she opened his fly, his cock blasted free. He wasn't wearing underwear.

"Forget something?" she asked, breathy as hell.

"I was in a hurry," he responded, breathier than hell.

Much too desperate, she curled her fingers around him. Not that she needed to for his sake. He was fully erect, the shaft long and thick, the head flaring.

Mercy, she thought. For both of them. "Please tell me you remembered to bring a condom."

"I brought lots." He dug into his pockets and produced an overflow of colorfully wrapped packets. They filled his hands like jewels, then began falling to the floor. He'd managed to cram what looked like the entire contents of a mixed-variety box into two shallow pockets.

"Jesus, Jay." She grabbed one before it hit the ground, not caring what type it was. "Put it on."

He discarded his beachy shoes and shoved his jeans down, pushing them past his hips and peeling them off. "You'd better not try to kick me out afterward."

Her head was spinning. "What?"

He finally took the condom and tore into it. "I need to stay the night. This is going to go too fast, and I want to do it right later."

Beverly pitched forward. Doing it right meant a slow, romantic buildup, and that wasn't the smorgasbord she'd had in mind. She'd bargained for hot and nasty. "You're not staying."

"Yes, I am."

She wanted to keep arguing, but he was already fitting himself with the rubber and she couldn't think past his penis. "Okay, damn it."

"That's my girl."

"Your former girl."

"Whatever."

He clutched her ass and thrust into her. In a manner of seconds, he was balls deep.

Beverly almost wept. Two years was a long time to go without. She should have been doing this all along. But not with him, she reminded herself. This was a one-night shot.

"Damn, you feel good." Jay pumped his hips, knocking her against the cabinet.

She heard plates and cups rattle. She heard the sound of her heart slamming against her rib cage, too. Out of a strange kind of fury, she bit the side of his neck.

"Leaving your mark?" he asked.

Was she? "I just need something to do with my mouth."

"You could kiss me."

"I'd rather bite." But she kissed him just the same, and their tongues tangled. He tasted wild and forbidden. She imagined that she tasted the same way to him. He was going after her with a vengeance.

When the kissing ended, he nudged her toward the kitchen table. Oh, God, she thought. Was he going to fuck her there?

Sure enough, he lifted her onto it.

"I'll make you breakfast tomorrow," he said.

"That isn't funny." Her bare bottom was sticking to the glass surface. "I'm never eating here again."

He laughed, albeit it roughly. "Open your legs, baby. Let me back inside."

She widened her thighs, and he climbed onboard and slid between them. She hoped the glass didn't shatter and cut them to shreds.

"You should still be my girl," he murmured against her ear.

As opposed to his former one? Talk about getting cut. "Don't go there."

"Sorry." He glanced down at their joined genitals. "I didn't mean to."

She looked down, too. Her nether lips were pink and swollen and filled with him. "You're forgiven."

He pushed deeper. "You aren't."

She knew he meant for divorcing him. If she had a lick of sense, she would've shoved him away. But it was too late for that, so she clawed his back and prayed for relief.

"Don't talk anymore," she told him.

"You, either."

"I won't." She couldn't, she thought.

He kissed her with brutal force and pummeled her hard and fast. Sex in a storm. Her brain fogged. Her vision blurred.

Then, heightening her haze, he dragged her right off the table and onto the floor, where they rolled around like mindless maniacs in a sea of colorful packets.

Positions kept changing, from her being on top, to him, to her, and back to him.

Beverly didn't know who came first. It might've happened at the same time. All she knew was that she was gasping for her next orgasmic breath, and he was arching and shuddering.

Afterward, he collapsed on top of her, and their sweaty bodies stuck together.

Seconds passed. Or was it a full minute?

Finally, he lifted his head and looked at her. They frowned at each other, their emotions raw.

He withdrew and removed the condom, tying it in a knot at the end. She gestured to the cabinet under the sink, letting him know where the trash was.

He got up and threw it away, and when he came back, he offered her a hand and helped her to her feet.

In spite of their obvious distress, his touch was gentle, and in the next dizzying moment, she was wrapped in his arms.

And lost in the feeling.

CHAPTER FOUR

Jay held Beverly for a while, and when he finally let go, his pulse tripped. She didn't appear to be faring any better. She looked bewildered, but he understood. Being together again seemed surreal.

Had he actually fucked her on the table, then dragged her to the floor? Clearly, this wasn't his finest hour.

"Take a bath with me," he said.

She gave him a baffled blink. "You take showers."

"I feel like a bath tonight."

"It makes you seem like David." She clarified. "He used to have his harem girls bathe him."

"Does that mean you're going to soap me down and wash my parts?"

"No."

For lack of a better reaction, he teased her. "Are you sure? I can kick back like a king."

"He was a prince."

"It was a figure of speech." And he felt the awkward need to explain. She seemed a bit too attached to David. "But I still want you to take a bath with me."

She finally softened to the idea. "I have some scented oil we can use."

To him, that sounded like a harem thing again, only it was nowhere near as appealing as getting bathed by a beautiful girl. Jay didn't relish the idea of being greasily perfumed, but he agreed because he didn't want to kill the mood.

The bathroom was decorated in cream and copper, with a paisley shower curtain and a fluffy rug. They filled the tub with warm water, and she added a few drops of oil from a small glass bottle.

"It's a natural blend," she said. "I made it myself."

"Really? When did you get into aromatherapy?"

"A few months ago."

Which, he surmised, was probably about the time she'd started getting regressed. "It smells spicy. Kind of like clove. Is that what's in it?"

"No. It's cinnamon bark."

"It's not so bad for a guy."

"Did you think I was going to use something flowery?"

"I wasn't sure."

Beverly turned toward the mirror, twisted her hair and clipped it on top of her head. But it was too heavy and a few pieces came loose.

"David smelled like sandalwood," she said.

He caught her gaze in the mirror and tried not to frown. "That's a good guy scent."

"Yes, it is." She dimmed the light switch, eased into the water and made room for him to sit across from her. It was a tight fit, but they managed to make it work, adjusting their legs accordingly. He left the shower curtain open, and air stirred softly across their skin.

"Maybe you can make some sandalwood shower gel for me to use at home," he said.

"So you can be like David?"

"You talk about him a lot." In his opinion, far more than she should.

"I can't help it. He was my husband."

Jay waved in front of her face. "I was your husband, Bev. *Me*, not *him*."

She shooed his hand away. "I didn't mean it like that."

"I know, but it sounded weird." And it fueled his jealousy. "What's the deal with him anyway? Why did he marry Camille?"

"It was arranged by their families. She'd been promised to him since they were children." Beverly sighed. "She used to daydream about him. She knew he had a harem, but she was naïve about it. After they were married, she wanted him to give up his other women."

An instant parallel struck, and he considered the similarity. "The way I wanted you to give up your dancing?"

"Yes, but she quit fighting his lifestyle and focused on loving him instead."

"So did it work out? Did David end up falling for her, too?"

"I don't know. I haven't gotten that far in my regression. But I researched them on the Internet and discovered that they had two children. A son and a daughter."

The fact she'd obtained historic information was spooky. It proved, he supposed, that David and Camille were real, making Beverly's past life seem real, too.

"If they had kids," he said, "then their relationship must have worked out."

"Not necessarily. The whole purpose of their marriage was to produce heirs, and that's what they did."

At some point, Jay had expected to raise a family with Beverly. He'd gone through the stage of thinking they were soul mates. Of course, he didn't really know what a soul mate was, other than an over-used expression.

He shifted his thoughts back to David and Camille. "What else did you find out?"

"Not much. Neylan doesn't exist anymore."

"Did David ever rule?"

"He became a sultan, like his father. I tried to find paintings of him and Camille in my research, but there weren't any."

"So all you have is what you see in your head?"

"Yes, but I think I could paint them if I were an artist. They're vivid to me."

Too vivid, he thought. He felt as if he were competing with David, only Jay didn't have a harem or a wife. He'd gotten screwed on both counts. "What about paintings of their kids?"

"I couldn't find any of those, either. All I know is that Neylan was conquered after their son's reign."

"It's all so strange."

"What is? My regression?"

"I don't think I'd want to be hypnotized. I don't think I'd want to know if I used to be someone else."

She gave him a curious look. "Wouldn't it be funny if you were David, if you got regressed and discovered you were him?"

"Yeah, right, funny. All I need is to be part of your past life." He considered the possibility and what sort of effect it would have, if any, on their current situation. "If I were him, would that make you more understanding of me in this life?"

"Of you expecting me to give up my dancing?" She shook

her head. "No, it wouldn't. I'm not giving up my empowerment for anyone."

"Fine. Then I'm keeping my harem."

"It was David's harem."

"If I used to be him, then it would've belonged to me, too."

She changed her tune. "Well, you weren't him."

He had no idea one way or the other, but he said, "I'll bet I was."

"You just want to claim all those beautiful girls."

"What's wrong with that?" For the hell of it, he flicked water at her. "So, tell me, did he get lots of blowjobs?"

She flicked back, spattering his chest. "You'd already know the answer to that if you were him."

"Okay, how's this for knowing the answer? He loved having his ladies go down on him. Maybe even two or three at a time, watching as they took turns."

"Shut up, Jay."

"I'm right, aren't I? That was his favorite thing. Lucky stiff."

Beverly rolled her eyes. "Lucky *stiff*?"

"That wasn't an innuendo." But he laughed anyway.

Surprisingly, so did she. But they sobered quickly.

"Let's go to bed," he said. By now the water had begun to cool, and he figured they needed warmth.

She agreed, and they got out of the tub and toweled off.

But before they retreated to her room, they headed for the kitchen-floor condoms.

As he gathered them, she winced and said, "I should sanitize the table."

He bit back a grin. "I'll do it in the morning before breakfast."

"I shouldn't be letting you stay here, let alone giving you stove privileges."

"You love my cooking."

"That's beside the point."

Beside the point or not, he was staying. They went to her room, and he dumped the prophylactics on the nightstand.

"Are you going to let me keep those?" she asked.

"Not unless you plan on inviting me back." He glanced at the ridiculous amount. "About twenty times."

"You wish."

Yeah, Jay thought, he did. But he shouldn't. "Get in bed and let me kiss you."

She looked suddenly panicked. "Is this where the 'do it right' part starts?"

"Just lie down and spread your legs." He loved the erotic texture of a smoothed woman, and she was fully waxed. "I'm starting there and working my way up."

She gave an anticipatory shiver. "You were always good at that." She turned down the bed and reclined, but she didn't open her legs.

He thought she looked modest, especially for a girl who pranced around in a G-string for a living. "Okay if I light this?" he asked about a candle on her dresser.

She nodded, and he used The Dusky Doll matches that were beside it. He then turned the lights low enough to complement the flame.

He crawled in bed and nuzzled her mound. Her shiver came back and her legs drifted open.

Anxious, he ran his tongue along her labia. She was already exposed, but he opened her a bit more.

She shifted her hips, lifting them in reflex, and he glanced up to see if she was watching. She was. He knew that when she came, she would fight to keep her eyes open. She would tug at his hair, too. Or at least that was what she used to do.

Had she changed? Was she different now?

He took another long, sweeping lick. She was already wet, and he was making her wetter. "I wonder, should I start calling you Princess?"

Her voice vibrated. "He didn't call her Princess. He called her Camille."

Ah, yes, David. His Royal Highness. The conversation had gone back to him. Jay wasn't sure how he felt about Camille's husband. Hell, he wasn't sure how he felt about himself.

All he knew was that Beverly tasted tangy and sweet. He swallowed her juices and moved his tongue to her clit. As he played with the tiny pink nub, he made it poke out.

Her stomach muscles fluttered, and he pressed his thumb into her pierced navel.

"Did the harem girls have belly jewels?" he asked.

"Some of them did. It was common then."

It was common now, too. But somehow it made her seem like one of David's slaves, even though she'd been the wife.

Annoyed by the other man's connection to her, Jay cupped her ass and brought her cunt closer to his mouth.

Feeling hot and hungry and possessive, he buried his face deeper, fucking her with his tongue and using his fingers on her clit.

Her breathing quickened, and she rocked forward. He took pleasure in knowing that she hadn't been with anyone since the divorce.

Even David couldn't take that away from him.

Beverly gasped and tugged on his hair. She was going to come the way she used to. She hadn't changed, not in that regard.

Her nerve endings exploded against him—a firework of spasms, a tightening of her inner muscles.

He waited for the shuddering to stop before he lifted his head. As promised, he kissed his way up, savoring her luscious curves.

He nipped on her hip bones, painted her stomach with his tongue, and gently sucked on each nipple, moving back and forth.

Curious, he checked out her expression and saw that her gaze was half-mast.

Finally, he put his mouth against hers, offering the taste that was on his lips. She sipped from him, and their tongues made slow, soft contact.

The kiss ended, and they separated, moving their bodies apart.

Yet somehow, they still seemed entwined.

~

My footsteps echoed as I walked down the corridor, my heart keeping hollow time.

A week had passed since our wedding night, and David had summoned me back to his bedchamber. I was alone. There was no need for Baki to escort me. I knew the way.

I reached David's door and opened it. I entered the lavish room and saw my husband. He was seated on the floor with a hookah pipe next to him. He stood up and came toward me. He was already half bare. All he wore were casual pants.

I, too, had donned lounging attire, wrapping myself in a delicately embroidered dressing gown.

He reached out and put a hand on my stomach, and I almost flinched. He seemed rather gentle.

"Do you think a child grows there?" he asked. "Do you think you conceived?"

"It is too early to tell."

"Do you have a feeling about it? An intuition?"

"No. I do not."

"Should we couple again?" he asked.

I got fluttery inside. "Do you want to?"

"Not particularly."

The sensations stopped. "Then we do not have to."

His hand remained on my stomach. "Maybe we should."

I realized then that he would be a caring father. But would he ever be a caring husband? Would I ever matter to him?

He mattered to me. I had been telling myself that I hated him, but deep down, I knew that I was capable of loving him, that the dream-silly girl I had once been refused to let go.

"We can do it swiftly," he said.

I did not want to do it swiftly. I wanted to sway with passion, to experience unbinding pleasure, to create it. But I was too uncomfortable to tell him how I felt.

Besides, how could I compete with his harem, with girls like Sarila and the exotic redhead?

"Remove your garment," he said.

I fumbled with the opening, wishing I knew how to strip seductively. If I was a harem girl, I would know everything.

I dropped the dressing gown and stood naked before him. He scanned the length of me and furrowed his brow. It was not the reaction for which I had hoped.

If only I had behaved better on our wedding night. If only I had not bruised his ego. But he had bruised mine, too.

"Turn around," he said.

I blinked, and he made a circular motion with his hands. I nodded and did his bidding.

He came up behind me. He smelled like sweetened smoke and his usual sandalwood spice.

I heard him lowering the waistband of his pants, and I exhaled as deeply as I could.

David moved closer and rubbed his penis against my bottom. Within seconds, he became erect, the silky length and bulbous crown stirring to life.

"Use your fingers to wet yourself," he said. "Put them in your mouth, then rub them inside."

My cheeks went hot. I had never done anything like that before. But I obeyed his command. I did not go very far inside. Still, I did the best I could. The feeling made my knees watery.

"Are you wet?" he asked.

"I think so."

"Then lean forward." His voice was rough.

I pressed against the wall in front of me, my hands flat against the surface. "Like this?"

"Yes."

He moved my hair away from my neck and the warmth of his breathing tickled my nape. Next, he slid his hands down my body and rested them at my hips. From there, he angled me, readying me for his penetration. I felt the tip of his penis at the opening of my vagina.

"It will be over soon," he said. "And this way you will not have to look at me while I am inside you."

Unsure of how to respond, I kept silent. I was afraid if I admitted that I was having affectionate feelings toward him and he scorned me, I would never recover.

He entered me, and I fanned my fingers against the wall. I noticed that the henna pattern on my hands was nearly gone.

He pushed deeper. Apparently I was wet enough to suit him. Luckily there was no pain. But unfortunately, no pleasure, either. All I felt was friction.

But then he placed his lips upon my neck, and my entire body tingled. I wanted to turn my head and attempt to kiss him. But I simply remained where I was and imagined that we were being ardent.

He pumped his hips, and all the while, he kept his mouth on my neck. I suspected that he wanted to bite my flesh, much in the way a stallion used his teeth on a mare.

But David refrained, keeping his mating instincts in check. If I had been one of his other women, he probably would have left wild marks on me.

I held tightly to the wall, and he spilled into me, bathing my womb.

Rather than withdraw, he stayed there, as if to ensure that I absorbed his seed.

But then he seemed to become aware of the quiet intimacy between us, and he backed away, leaving me bereft.

I did not turn around, as I could not bear to look at him. He lifted my dressing gown from the floor and draped it over my shoulders.

"You may go now," he said.

Still facing the wall, I got dressed, and without casting a glance in his direction, I left his bedchamber, wondering how I was going to survive my marriage.

CHAPTER FIVE

Beverly knew this wasn't a good time to dwell on the sanctity of marriage, not while she was in bed with her ex, but her thoughts kept drifting toward holy matrimony.

Or unholy, considering Jay's ménage.

She found herself asking, "Why did you exchange fake vows with Amber and Luke?"

He shifted onto his side. "You want to talk about that now?"

Yes, now, in the height of being warm and slick and naked. It was stupid, she knew, but curiosity had gotten the best of her.

"I did it to forget about us," he said. "Our vows, our honeymoon night."

"Did it work?"

"Apparently not." His laugh was humorless, but it wasn't bitter. He sounded lost.

She knew how he felt. "We had quite a wedding, didn't we?"

"Yeah. Barefoot on the beach with the sun setting in the sky." He crinkled his forehead. "It almost seems corny now."

"No, it doesn't." In spite of the outcome, she still considered it the most idyllic day of her life. "We just couldn't make the rest of it work. That happens to a lot of people."

He leaned on his elbow. "You're in a reflective mood."

"I know, and I shouldn't be. This is supposed to be about sex."

"We're not done in that regard. We've still got more dirty-sweet stuff to do."

She should have smiled, but her reflective mood hadn't passed. "As sweet and dirty as the things you and Luke did to Amber?"

He lifted his eyebrows. "You want details?"

"I don't know. Maybe." At the moment, she was struck by his expression. It reminded her of David. He was always raising his brows at Camille.

Was it possible that they were the same man? At times, they seemed to share similar qualities, maybe even the same spirit, and at other times, they couldn't be more different.

Comparing them probably wasn't a good idea, but inviting Jay into her bed hadn't been a good idea, either.

Yet here she was, fixated on him.

"I'll tell you, if you want to know," he said. "But I'd rather not if it's going to upset you."

"It won't." Would it? She hoped not. "I'm not the jealous type," she added for independent measure. "Or not usually."

"That's true."

Yes, she thought. Between the two of them, he was far more possessive. But she got surges of it. She wasn't infallible. "So, are you going to tell me?"

Jay obliged. "The dynamics were strange from the start. Although Luke went along with having a threesome, what he really wanted was to keep Amber for himself. Me, I was just trying to fill my head with sex." He paused, grinned. "Both heads."

She playfully punched his arm, and they laughed. But they quieted quickly.

Beverly then said, "I want to know about the honeymoon." Sex was the topic of the night. But so was marriage.

"It was crazy," he responded. "Two masked men and a woman in a wedding gown. It didn't cure me of my divorce ills, but I liked being part of it. It was exciting to be around Luke and Amber while they were falling in love."

She tried to envision what he was describing. She'd never imagined having a conversation of this magnitude. "Where did it take place?"

"In a bungalow at the Chateau Marmont."

Ah, she thought, the decadent hotel above the Sunset Strip. "That fits."

"Amber chose the location. She was already there when Luke and I arrived. We brought sex toys with us, all kinds of kinky stuff. There was cake and champagne, too. But the first thing we did was have the ceremony."

"The vows?"

He nodded. "We led her to the bedroom and blindfolded her, and once she was on her knees, Luke told her to recite the vows so she could be our wife."

Their *wife*. Hearing him say it in that context made her homesick for being his bride. But she did her darnedest to will it away. "Go on."

"After she said the vows, Luke stepped in front of her and unzipped his pants."

Beverly blinked. "While she was blindfolded and on her knees?"

"That was the point. He handed her a cock ring to seal the deal, and she put it on him and gave him head."

"Oh, my God. Please tell me you didn't do that, too."

"Sorry, but I did."

"*Jay.*" She could do little more than gape at him.

"You said you wanted to know." He moved closer. "Besides, don't you think it's just a little bit sexy?"

She did, heaven help her, but she hated to admit it. "I'm not that kinky."

"Bullshit. You strip in front of strangers just about every night. You fulfill men's fantasies and you get off on it."

She drew a sharp breath. "I don't want to argue about my dancing." They'd done way too much of that in the past.

"Who's arguing?" He climbed on top of her, and his cock went magnificently hard.

She waited for him to open her legs and thrust into her, but he didn't. Then again, he couldn't, or wouldn't, not without a condom, and he hadn't grabbed a packet off the nightstand. Instead he pinned her hands above her head, gripping her wrists, and stared down at her.

"What are you doing?" she asked.

"Taking control."

She felt awkward and vulnerable. But oddly aroused, too. "Of me?"

"I told you we still had more dirty-sweet stuff to do."

She gazed at the wall of his chest. All male and muscle, but free of hair. He kept it shaved for photo shoots. She glanced lower. He had hair down there, but it was neatly trimmed. Manscape.

He said, "Maybe I should kneel over your face."

That would definitely qualify as dirty. She wasn't sure about sweet, though. Regardless, she wet her lips. She envisioned sucking him straight into her mouth.

"Or maybe I should fuck you between your tits."

More dirty. Her nipples went holy-hell hot. When he leaned forward to lick one of them, she shivered.

"You can do whatever you want," she told him.

He lifted his head. "Can I make a sundae?"

That threw her. "What?"

"All over your body. Ice cream, syrup, whipped cream and maraschino cherries." He smiled and bumped his balls against her inner thigh. "A couple of nuts, too."

Ha, she thought. Now he was talking dirty-sweet, literally, metaphorically.

Her shiver intensified. The nipple he'd licked puckered in the air, the areola crinkled and flushed.

He seemed pleased by what he saw and treated her other breast to the same sensitive delight.

Afterward, he asked, "Do you have any of that stuff?"

"No." She didn't keep dessert fixings around, but now she wished that she did.

"We'll do it next time."

"There isn't supposed to be a next time. We're having a one-nighter."

"There's too much to do in one night. You'll have to invite me back."

"For a sundae?"

"Yeah. Maybe even on Sunday. After church."

"You know I'm not a churchgoer anymore." Even if her parents still preached at her plenty.

"Yeah, but a little prayer never hurt anyone."

She was praying now. The way he affected her was dangerous. Her arms were still raised above her head, and her clit was peeking out of her pussy. The temptation to rub it made her twitch. If only she could use her hands. She would rub and rub and let him watch.

He reprimanded her. "Quit squirming around."

"Then quit torturing me."

"I'm not doing anything but trying to keep you still."

"Exactly."

He'd never played these types of games with her before, but he'd never been her one-night stand. He almost seemed like a stranger.

"I think I'll just fuck you the regular way," he said.

To leave her wanting more? To prod her into inviting him back again? To secure his nasty-boy place in her bed?

She glanced at the candle he'd lit earlier. The flame cast jittery shadows on the wall. "I don't care what you do, just do it."

He released her and leaned over to get a condom, a position that put his cock wildly close to her face.

He gave her the packet. "Put it on."

Beverly did what he told her to do, and his penis jerked from the attention. He remained close to her face.

But only long enough for her to catch her breath.

He slid down, putting them hip to hip. Thick and hard, he plunged into her. But before setting his pace, he latched onto her wrists and lifted her arms above her head once again.

Rocking his pelvis, he went deeper. He tightened his grip, too. She was at his mercy. Like a newly christened harem girl, she thought. Or an ex-wife turned sex slave.

His upper body bore down on hers, and the compression sent bursts of air from her lungs.

His shaft worked like a piston, drilling her into the bed. Taking what she could, she lifted her legs in an acrobatic pose and angled her hips, forcing his rigorous motion to bump her clit.

"Agile," he muttered.

"Dancer," she reminded him.

"Stripper," was his rough reply.

Did he like that she was using her skills to pump up the heat? The same skills that encompassed the job he'd wanted her to quit?

She imagined leaving marks down his back, but she couldn't break free to claw him. Then again, maybe she didn't really want to. The pressure of being pinned into place felt maniacally good.

She glanced at the candle again. Wax pooled in the center and melted hungrily over the sides.

He lowered his head to French-kiss her, and she welcomed the taste of his tongue. She couldn't think beyond the lust.

She moaned through the kiss, and it sounded like a deep, dark plea, even to her.

Jay disengaged their mouths and positioned himself so she

could watch. Her labia swelled as he moved in and out, her cream coating him. At the top of her wide-open lips, her clit stood out like a tiny spear, and every time he bumped it, she gasped. He drove himself harder and faster, filling her with warm, wet friction.

He arched his muscle-ripped torso and his cock spasmed. In response, she went gloriously tight beneath him, wrapping her legs around his waist and lifting her butt in the air.

"Fuck," he said.

Yes, *fuck*, she thought, as they shattered at the same time, convulsing and shaking in carnal greed.

Struggling to keep her sanity, she counted the aftershocks. One, two, three . . .

Once the final quake subsided, he pulled out, let go of her arms, and dropped down on top of her. He gleamed with sweat.

He nuzzled her neck, and Beverly held him. She caressed his spine, too, tracing the vertebrae with the tips of her fingers.

Steeped in intimacy, in afterglow, she wondered how a divorced couple could get this close.

"You smell good," he said, voice muffled against her skin.

She skimmed another vertebra, moving softly, slowly, keeping a languid pace. "I smell like sex."

"And cinnamon bark."

Ah, yes, from the bath. She pressed her nose to his shoulder and inhaled remnants of it on him, too.

Together, they breathed each other in. She considered ending the tender madness and telling him to get off of her, but the impulse to keep him was greater.

After a bit of time passed, she hoped he hadn't fallen asleep that way. The weight of his body would give her a cramp. Besides, he was still wearing the condom. If it slackened against his flaccid penis and leaked, it would make a mess.

"Jay?"

"What?" He lifted his head. He wasn't asleep. He'd responded too quickly.

"You'd better get rid of the rubber."

"Oh, yeah. Shit, I forgot." He grinned like an irresponsible schoolboy.

God, he was cute. Of course, he hadn't been cute when he'd been ramming her into the bed.

He reached down and took care of his guy business. "Good thing I wasn't still inside you."

She didn't respond, other than to give a quick nod. All she needed was his beautiful little baby. How would that be for a messed-up divorce?

He went into the bathroom, and she flattened her palms over her tummy, feeling uncomfortably maternal.

Jay returned and caught her deep in thought.

"What's wrong?" he asked. "Do you have a stomachache? Are you sick?"

"No. I just . . ." Just what? She dropped her hands. But she didn't drop the topic in her mind. "Did you ever think about having children?"

"When we were together?" He shifted his naked stance. "Yes, and I assumed that we would have them someday."

"I thought that, too." She made a face. "But why didn't we ever talk about it?"

"It was just one of those givens, I guess. Something we thought would happen when the time was right. Does it matter now? Talking about it wouldn't have saved our marriage."

"No, of course not." Children hadn't been the problem.

He didn't rejoin her in bed. He just stood there in his long, lean, gorgeous birthday suit, intensifying an already awkward moment.

Then he asked, "Do you have an extra toothbrush I could use? I didn't bring anything with me." He glanced at the stack of condoms. "Except those."

"I have an unused travel toothbrush. It's in a little container in the medicine chest. Here, I'll show you."

While in the bathroom with him, she felt married again. She cautioned him about squeezing the toothpaste tube from the middle because that was his habit, and she was fanatical about rolling it from the end.

But at least by the time they took turns spitting into the sink and returned to bed, they were both minty fresh.

Once they were under the covers, he reached for her, and she curled up beside him the way she used to.

He gave her a chaste good-night kiss, then said, "Don't forget, I'm cooking in the morning."

"I remember." Much too attached, she closed her eyes, struggling to shut off her heart-pinging memories and go to sleep.

But all she could feel was him, strong and warm, by her side.

~

Beverly awakened to a delicious aroma. She squinted into the light and sat up, her senses on familiar alert.

She got out of bed and put on a plain white robe, then went into the bathroom to freshen up, taking a few minutes to get her physical and emotional self together.

Preparing for the sight of Jay in chef mode, she squared her shoulders.

What a night, she thought. And what a morning-after. She was nervous to see him.

What would happen when she entered the kitchen? Would she fall prey to their married past?

No, she thought. No matter what he said or did, she wasn't going to let him affect her.

Determined to keep her cautious-girl wits, she followed the tantalizing scent. There he was, at the stove, wearing the jeans and T-shirt she'd helped peel off of him last night.

Apparently he'd sanitized the table, because it was already set with her everyday plates, glasses and flatware.

She stepped farther into the room, and he turned and flashed his signature smile. Her knees went wobbly. So much for not being affected.

"Hi," he said.

"Hi," she repeated.

"I was going to wake you soon."

"You were?"

He nodded, and several beats of silence passed. She wished that she'd gotten fully dressed instead of being naked beneath a robe. Her other robe, the luxurious one that made her feel like Camille, was still heaped near the front door where Jay had dropped it. Another sexy reminder of last night, she thought.

"Coffee?" he asked.

"Sure." She hoped that she sounded more relaxed than she felt. "But I can get it myself."

Beverly approached the coffeepot, and he handed her a cup. She thanked him, and he leaned forward and kissed her hotly on the mouth. She almost forgot to breathe.

He stared at her afterward, then said, "I'm making spinach, tomato and feta cheese omelets. Pancakes, too." He indicated the flapjacks on the griddle.

She tried for an upbeat tone. "Everything looks great." She poured her coffee and added milk, careful not to splash it. Her hands were unsteady. She wanted him to kiss her again.

Why? So she could quit breathing all the way?

"Take a seat," he told her. "It's almost done."

Yes, she thought. Sit. Behave. She carried her coffee over to the table and plunked down in a chair.

Nonetheless, she was faltering. Beverly didn't feel like herself. But she hadn't been herself when she'd allowed Jay to come over last night, either.

So, who had she been? Camille?

He brought syrup, margarine and salt and pepper to the table, then filled their water glasses and served the food. He'd done well with the ingredients he'd found in her fridge. She wouldn't have thought to put feta cheese in the eggs. She'd bought it to use as a salad topping.

Jay joined her, and they simultaneously reached for the syrup. He smiled and let her go first.

This time, the familiar tilt of his lips made her heart wobble. She would've preferred jittery knees.

"What are you going to do today?" he asked.

She drenched her pancakes and handed him the bottle. "I have to work this afternoon."

"I thought you didn't like day shifts. You always said the money was better at night."

"I'm not going to the club today. I teach striptease, lap and pole dancing at a studio. To regular women," she clarified.

"You took a second job?"

"It's only one day a week."

"Hmmm."

She frowned, his reaction giving her pause. "What's that supposed to mean?"

"I guess I'm just wondering if teaching is your way of trying to legitimize what you do at The Doll."

She shouldered his criticism. Or at least she tried to. "I don't need to legitimize anything."

"I think you do. Most people don't respect strippers, but they respect teachers."

What he said was true, and it jabbed at her like a dull knife. Exotic dancers rarely admitted what they did for a living. But a dance instructor, even one who taught striptease, could speak easily of it.

Then again, that wasn't always the case. Her parents didn't like either of her jobs.

But she didn't mention that. Instead she sat back and rehashed the situation in her mind. Beverly came from an ultra-conservative family, and as a child she'd been plain and unassuming, a proper little girl who danced in average ballet recitals.

But as soon as she began to overdevelop and garner attention, her parents behaved as if it was her fault, cautioning her on how to dress, on how to downplay her buxom body. So much so, she'd spent her youth in a state of self-consciousness. Even her early twenties had been awkward.

Then, at the law firm where she'd been plodding along as a receptionist, a high-powered female client had introduced her to a club owner, and Beverly fell headfirst into what she'd been trying to avoid.

But once she'd embraced her hot-blonde appeal and entered the strip scene, she felt remarkably free. Her curves were no longer a curse. She was getting paid to be ogled, and she liked it. She even made her breasts bigger.

Jay interrupted her thoughts. "Do you enjoy teaching?"

"Yes, very much."

"Then why don't you do it full-time?"

"And give up stripping?"

"It's something to consider."

"Why? Because you're back in my bed? Because my dancing bothers you?"

He shrugged, but they both already knew the answer. He was doing what he'd done during their marriage, only in a calmer, quieter way. Yet somehow the lack of argument was just as painful.

As the silence mounted, he asked, "So *am* I back in your bed? Are you going to keep seeing me?" He reached across the table for her hand. "Or did I just blow it?"

She struggled for a response. "I want to keep seeing you, but not if you're going to keep dredging up all of that old stuff."

"I won't do that anymore."

"Promise?"

"Yes. Absolutely." He curled his fingers around hers. "We'll have a no-dredge affair."

"Okay," she said, a bit reluctantly, and let out the breath she was holding. She was still going to be careful. She couldn't bear to repeat their mistakes. Nor did she think it was possible to fix what had been broken.

Not in this life.

CHAPTER SIX

Baki looked at me as if I were mad. Maybe I was.

I had summoned him to my apartment, and now we were in my garden, discussing my plan. I wanted to disguise my appearance and infiltrate my husband's harem, posing as his newest slave girl. If I could not disband his harem, I decided that the best course of action was to become part of it.

The eunuch shook his head. "It will never work."

"Why not?" I argued. I longed to entice David, to make him ache for me, but I was too inexperienced to know what to do, and he remained too distant to notice that I cared.

Baki spoke. "How can you become a slave girl? A slave lives in the harem, under guard."

"I already considered that."

"*And how do you see a way past it?*"

"*I can sneak back and forth between this apartment and the harem. I can play both roles. But the other girls will have to protect my secret.*" I tried to sound light and free, certain of my plan. "*It is a masquerade we can all be part of, and once I tell my husband the truth, he will be enthralled by it.*"

Baki tensed his beefy arms. He looked especially bulky today, but maybe it was because he was standing next to a planter of yellow flowers. "*What if the prince is not enthralled?*"

"*He will be,*" I insisted, when in fact I had no idea how David would react.

"*He could beat us for our deception. Kill us, if he was inclined.*"

By us, Baki meant everyone who was involved, including me. Of course my death would have political consequences. Still, I tried not to shudder. "*Is he vicious? Is he violent with you? Or with the girls?*"

"*No. But this might invoke his anger.*"

I did not want to think of David lashing out at them because of me. "*I will take full responsibility. I will tell him that I ordered all of you to help me. I am a member of the royal household, after all.*"

"*Yes, Your Highness.*" Baki managed a dutiful nod. "*I mean no offense, but I fear it will be a challenge turning a European princess into a slave.*"

"*No offense taken.*"

86

"*You realize that you will have to refer to the prince as* Master, *and that you will be required to succumb to his every desire.*"

"*I am aware of what my requirements will be.*" Or as aware as a barely knowledgeable bride could be.

He remained in sight of the sunny blooms. "*I will have to choose the right girl to instruct you.*"

"*Only one girl? I would rather have two. Sarila and her friend. The redhead.*" I thought they made a unique pair, and I was curious to know more about them.

"*If they are the instructors you want, then they shall be at your disposal. They can also help create a new identity for you. You will need an engaging name and a believable background.*" He angled his head. "*Altering your appearance will be a challenge. If the prince recognizes you, your plot will be doomed.*"

"*Then we shall devise a clever disguise.*"

"*Yes, we shall.*"

"*I want to be the most exquisite girl in the harem,*" I proclaimed. "*The most accomplished dancer, too.*"

"*If that is what you wish.*"

"*It is.*" If I failed to shine above the rest, then what would be the point?

Baki said, "*You may be called upon to dance at private celebrations. The prince always chooses his best girls to entertain his guests.*"

My heart bumped my chest. "What kinds of guests?"

"Influential men. Other royals and the like."

Oh, my, I thought. "We will have to figure a way out of that."

"If you become a slave there will not be a way out of it. You will do your master's bidding." The eunuch stood strong and still. "Perhaps you would prefer to rethink your masquerade."

"You mean abolish it?" A sudden burst of light glared through the trees, making me squint. The palace walls were high, but the sun still made its appearance. I moved to the other side of the bench, taking to the shade.

"Maybe it would be best to abandon your quest," he prodded. "If you are uncertain," he added kindly.

"My decision stands." I would do what had to be to done to win my husband's favor, to become his most prized possession, even if it meant dancing for other men.

Baki finally accepted my determination. He, of all people, knew that I was at odds with my lackluster marriage.

"I suggest that we get started," he said. "We have much to do to ensure your success."

~

Baki escorted me to the harem, and my excitement mounted. He rounded up the women and other eunuchs, and once they were gathered in the great hall of the main building, he told them of my plan.

Nonetheless, he downplayed the danger I was putting myself in. In fact, he presented it as a bit of naughty fun, calling it "a secret sex game" their master was sure to enjoy.

Curious chatter and girlish giggles erupted, but all went silent when he warned them that anyone who gossiped about it outside the harem walls would be tortured.

He also claimed that I, Her Royal Highness, would choose the method of torture and that he, the head curator, would inflict said punishment.

He sounded quite convincing, and at that moment I realized how loyal Baki was to me. He was doing his best to protect me, to make certain that David did not accidentally discover my masquerade before I was ready to reveal myself to him.

When Baki informed Sarila and the redhead—whose name was Ruby—that they had been chosen as my instructors, they smiled appreciatively. As for the rest of the girls, some seemed jealous that they had not been picked and others seemed relieved. If I had been in their position, I was uncertain how I would have felt.

Baki escorted Sarila, Ruby and me to the wardrobe room, which was crammed with lavish attire. I caught sight of breast bridles, as well as other oddly enticing accessories.

"This is not daily harem wear," Baki said. "It is reserved for nights with the master."

I nodded my understanding, and from there, we continued

to a community dressing room, where vanity tables were artfully positioned.

There was also a row of sunken tubs. A harem girl must bathe often, I was told. She was always expected to be clean and fresh.

Next to the tubs was a toiletry area, with bottles of oils, various liquids, containers of sea sponges and pots of honey, each labeled with an identifying flavor.

"The honey is to make us sweet for the master," Sarila said, when she noticed me scanning the labels on the pots.

"Down there," Ruby added, in her British voice. She motioned to her pubis, which was covered today. Both girls were dressed in lounging attire.

Regardless, I envisioned them naked and dabbing the gooey substance between their legs. Then I envisioned myself doing it, recalling David's remark about his skilled tongue.

My cheeks went hot. "Does the master have a favorite flavor?"

Sarila shook her head. "He says they taste different on different girls."

Baki spoke. "We need to create a background for Her Highness and give her a harem name."

Ruby said, "I was given my name for my hair."

"Mine means waterfall," Sarila offered. "It was chosen for me because I move fluidly, like water."

Yes, I thought, she did. I suspected that David enjoyed her

carnal swaying. I was intrigued yet envious. These women were my competition, along with all of the others.

"Maybe you should choose your own name," Ruby said, paying me the respect that was due.

As much as I appreciated her suggestion, I wanted to be named in the customary way. "I would prefer that someone else choose it."

"I think you are as elegant as a flower," Sarila said.

"So do I," Ruby chimed. "Something long-stemmed."

"A rose?" Baki asked.

The women shook their heads. "Too common," Sarila explained.

Baki tried again. "A lily, a tulip."

Again, heads were shaken.

"She is elegant, but clever, too," Ruby said. "A princess masquerading as a slave. Sweet and potent, like a poppy."

Sarila tapped her chin. "We could call her Afyon. For the black castle opium region."

Afyon, I thought. It made me feel exotic already. "I like it."

Baki appeared satisfied, as well. "I will tell the master that she was named for her sweet potency. He will be aroused by that."

Ruby grinned. "He'll probably want to smoke her in his pipe."

"And drug himself with her kisses," Sarila added.

I touched a finger to my lips. David had yet to kiss me, and I was anxious to feel his mouth upon mine.

"Now, onto your background," the eunuch said to me.

I redirected my focus. "I can be French. I speak the language. I can mimic the accent, too."

"That will do nicely. He has no other French girls."

Sarila perked up. "That will make the master even more excited to kiss you." She stuck out her tongue and wiggled it. "The French kiss like this."

Ruby giggled and stuck out hers, too.

Baki rolled his eyes and returned to the business at hand, conjuring my pre-harem life. "I will keep it simple and say that you were captured by pirates on a ship bound for the colonies, then sold to a trader."

Ruby added to my fictitious tale. "You were a young widow on her way to become an indentured servant."

I understood that I needed a respectable reason for not being a virgin, but I was uncertain about being an indentured servant. "What happens to wealthy women who are captured?" I asked. "Or those of noble birth?"

"They are held for ransom," Sarila answered. "Only the poor become slaves."

I wondered how she and Ruby had met their fate, but I did not query them about it. Instead I asked, "Would it be plausible if I were educated?" Posing as an unschooled commoner would be difficult for me. "Maybe I was indentured as a tutor?"

Baki agreed that education would suit my character, and my new identity was finalized. Altering my appearance was another matter.

While I sat at a mirrored vanity, my instructors tested various hairstyles and cosmetics, and although I looked quite fetching, I still looked like me.

Finally, Sarila said, "I think we should use a plant-mixture on your hair to give it a reddish hue. That will make a significant difference, and you can wash it out each time."

"I have an idea, too." This from Ruby. "We should design the kohl around your eyes to look like a ball mask. We can attach jewels and feathers and all sorts of pretty ornaments."

Intrigued, I asked, "Attach them how?"

"With spirit gum. It is an adhesive used in theater, and it goes directly on your skin. We can chart a fancy new mask for every costume you wear."

Baki stood back and listened. Then he said, "Feathers might tickle the master's stomach when she kneels between his legs."

"Yes, but I think he will like it." Ruby organized a tray of blue, black and green kohl. "Her attempt at intrigue will make his cock hard."

I refrained from clearing my throat. I had never imagined a woman saying that word and certainly not in reference to my husband. But I decided that I had better learn to accept it.

"I agree with Ruby," Sarila said. "The master will appreciate Her Highness's creativity."

"*Afyon*," *I corrected quickly. It would be disastrous for the other girls to speak my title in front of the prince.* "*Refer to me by that name to get used to it.*"

"*Yes, Afyon,*" *she said with a slight bow, then caught herself. Slaves did not bow to each other.*

"*You must remember to comply, too,*" *I told Baki.* "*You cannot favor me over the other girls. Otherwise, His Highness, the master,*" *I amended,* "*might wonder why.*"

Ever loyal, the eunuch promised to abide by me. But regardless, he encountered a problem with my charade. "*What if the master tires of your masquerade? Or what if he wants you to bathe with him? Bathing will require you to remove your painted mask.*"

I sighed. "*Your concerns are warranted. My disguise needs to be foolproof.*"

Ruby interjected. "*Maybe Baki can tell the master that you are injured beneath the mask.*" *She conjured details.* "*When your ship was seized, you were caught in a scuffle and took a nasty cut near one of your eyes. And, now, while it is the process of healing, you devised a way to make yourself pretty for the master.*"

I turned to Baki. "*Do you think that will work?*"

"*Yes, I do. Especially if I tell the master how eager you are to serve him. That once the cut heals and you appear to him without a mask, he will be awed by your true beauty.*"

"*At least that part is genuine,*" *Sarila said.* "*She is eager, and once he discovers who she is and the measures she took to please him, he will be awed."*

I hoped and prayed that they were right, that David would be entranced by me.

"Shall we create your new look and present you to the rest of the harem for their reaction?" Ruby asked.

I nodded, and they went about mixing the plant dye for my hair. Once it had been applied and the temporary color took hold, I was required to bathe and rinse.

I motioned for Baki to turn his back, but he remained where he was.

"If you are going to impersonate a harem girl," he said, "you cannot be shy around the eunuchs, especially the head curator. The first time I present you to the master, you will be expected to strip for him, and I will be standing nearby. You cannot avoid being naked in my presence."

Oh, goodness, I thought. "What else will happen that first time?"

"He will decide if he wants to keep you."

My mouth fell agape. "Are you saying that he can reject me?"

"Of course he can. But I do not see why he would. Not unless you are too timid for his tastes."

Challenged by Baki's remark, I loosened my caftan and let it fall to the floor. I was not going to allow my shyness to be an obstacle. If David rejected me, I would surely die.

While I bathed, Sarila and Ruby told me about their experiences at the slave market where Baki had initially purchased them.

"We were ordered to disrobe and he examined us from all sides," Sarila said.

"He opened our mouths and checked our teeth," Ruby added. She leaned in close. "He even put his fingers inside of us. But he does that all the time now."

"He does?" I did my best to hide my shock.

"Yes, but not for sexual purposes. Whenever we are called to the master, Baki sees to our contraceptive needs. He inserts the sponges into us so that we do not forget."

I said, "That will not be necessary with me."

Ruby furrowed her brow. "I wonder if the master will be able to detect that you are not wearing a sponge."

Sarila interjected, "If he could detect them, forgetting to insert them would not be such an issue. The master would check for himself."

I decided that Sarila was the smarter of the two, but that Ruby had a stronger imagination.

After I rinsed, Sarila offered me a cloth in which to dry. I used one on my hair, as well.

Ruby searched the wardrobe room for something for me to wear. She reappeared with a provocative outfit and helped me into it.

A sheer top barely covered my breasts, and loose, filmy

pants were slit along the sides and dipped low in front with a jangling belt. Adding a touch of exotic glamour, she pasted a gem inside of my navel, using the spirit gum she had mentioned earlier.

Sarila styled my hair, entwining ribbon around the silky strands, and Ruby designed a painted mask that enhanced my clothes, adding sparkling jewels and elaborate feathers.

Upon completion, I could only stare. I was no longer me, no longer recognizable.

Baki came up behind me and gazed at my transformed reflection. "Afyon is a creature to behold." He turned to compliment the girls. "Your work is brilliant."

They beamed from his praise and paraded me around the harem, showing me off to the other girls. I was treated like a princess, but of course that was what I was. Had I actually been a new harem girl, envy probably would have run amok. At second glance, I did notice a few jealous faces. But that was better, I thought. I needed all of this to appear quite real, and so far, my dress rehearsal was a success.

"When are you going to tell the master about Afyon?" Ruby asked Baki.

"Yes, when?" Sarila parroted.

"I will request an audience with him for tomorrow. Perhaps in the morning at the stable before he rides. He favors that time for meetings."

"I want to be there," I said.

Baki responded, "I cannot bring Afyon. Not until he agrees to see her."

"No. No. Me, Her Highness, his wife. I want to hear what is being said."

"That is your prerogative," he told me. "But I wonder how His Highness will feel about you lurking about while I discuss a new harem girl."

"I suspect that he will not like it. But then, maybe he will. I am willing to take the chance."

And experience David's reaction firsthand.

CHAPTER SEVEN

In the morning, I arrived at the stables. The stable boys and grooms reacted respectfully. My husband, however, did not look pleased to see me.

He spotted me petting the nose of one of his prized Arabians, a breed known for its powerful endurance. They carried their tails high and proud, but they also had uniquely shaped heads. I thought they were magnificent.

I kept petting the stallion and received a scowl from David. He walked over to me, and I took a quick breath. The Arabian snorted. I smiled to myself, thinking the horse was supporting me.

"What are you doing here?" David asked.

My heart pounded at an unmerciful pace. He looked im-

posing in his riding attire, tall and wicked, with a whip in his hand. I was dressed modestly, with a veil covering my hair.

"I enjoy this environment," I said, then swiftly inquired about the stallion. "What is his name?"

"Brave One."

"Ah, so he was named for his courage. Splendid."

David slanted the horse a traitorous glance. The valiant Arabian appeared to like me. He nuzzled my hand like a naughty boy sniffing out the scent of a pretty girl.

The prince said, "A princess should not loiter about the stables."

"I am not loitering." In Neylan, horsemanship was mostly reserved for men. But the European influence on the culture did not forbid women from making their equine mark, if they so dared. "I might ride today."

"Not with me" was his reply.

"I did not say I was joining you" was mine. I waited a moment, then ventured to say, "I heard talk of a new harem girl."

"So that is why you are here, to spy on my upcoming meeting with Baki."

"If I were spying, I would be lurking in a corner somewhere."

"To insinuate yourself, then."

"I have a right to be curious."

He adjusted the whip in his hand. "This was not on my agenda. I did not request a new girl."

Oh, no, I thought. I had hoped for more interest on his part. But I could not allow him to think that I was encouraging him to increase the size of his harem.

I said, "I suppose a man gets weary."

"Of what?"

"Having too many women to please."

There went his brows, shooting upward, but I expected as much. I had just mocked his virility.

"The purpose of a harem is for the man's pleasure. But I could own hundreds of girls and still perform with two or three a night."

"Oh, my. Really?" I turned to Brave One and said, "And I thought you were the stud."

The horse nickered, and I bit back a smile. I thought it was a suitable reaction.

David, naturally, was not amused. Someday I hoped to hear my husband laugh, for him to appreciate my silly sense of humor. But for now, keeping him focused on the new girl was what mattered.

I turned and saw Baki, realizing it was time for the meeting. David turned, too, and the head curator stood back and waited for the prince to approach him.

When my husband moved forward, I fell into step with him. He did not shoo me away, so I kept his long-limbed pace.

As we walked, my veil fluttered in the breeze. I had to wash my hair three times yesterday to rid it of its reddish sheen, but I did not mind. To me, Afyon's disguise was worth the trouble.

Baki bowed to us, and David waved an impatient hand, causing the eunuch to right his posture. In the background, Brave One nickered again, and it struck me how men in this region were castrated, yet horses were not.

When Baki glanced at me, David said, "I am allowing her to eavesdrop."

The eunuch did not react. But he was too invested in our scheme to give away his thoughts.

He said, "The new girl is called Afyon, named for her sweet potency."

My husband seemed intrigued. "Tell me more."

"She is yet untrained."

"So she was not acquired from another harem?"

"I purchased her from a trader."

"Then she is untouched?"

"No, Your Highness, she is a young widow. But she is eager to be your slave, anxious to learn the ways of pleasuring a prince."

"As she should be," David remarked.

"Yes, of course. But she is also a girl of wild imaginings."

David angled his head. He seemed intrigued again. "How so?"

"She requested to be presented to you in disguise." Baki went on to explain how Afyon had come to be injured and

how she hoped to entice her new master by wearing elaborate masks until she healed.

My husband fell silent, and I feared that a disguised slave did not appeal to him. I wanted to make eye contact with Baki, to prod him into singing more of Afyon's praises, but the eunuch's gaze was downcast.

Baki finally spoke again. "She is of French origin, with a lilting voice. Intelligent, too. She has been rapidly learning our language, studying diligently so she may better serve you."

David turned to me. "What do you think?"

"Me?" I nearly swallowed my tongue.

"You are the nosy wife. Do you want to be there when she is presented to me?"

"Of course not!" I tried for a tone of indignation. Being at the presentation would be impossible. Just the mere thought made me panic. "You know how I feel about your harem."

"Then maybe it would behoove you to stay out of my business," he chided, and shifted his attention back to Baki. "You may present Afyon this afternoon, after my midday meal. But I warn you, she had better be as eager and alluring as you claim she is."

"You will not be disappointed," the eunuch said.

After that, he was dismissed, and my plight was clear. It had become even more crucial that Afyon impress the prince.

I spent the rest of the day in the harem, preparing for my presentation.

"You must kneel before the master with your gaze lowered," Sarila told me.

"Then stand and disrobe upon his command," Ruby added.

I listened to their instruction and tried to envision the scenario they described. What if he found me lacking? What if I was too nervous to entice him?

I fretted about my wardrobe. "I do not want to wear the outfit from yesterday." Although I wanted to look wildly fetching, I was worried about fumbling with a tiny top or tripping over a pair of billowy pants. "I would prefer something that is equally alluring but simpler to remove."

Ruby prepared my bath. "You will be wrapped in a cloth."

"A cloth?" That was far too simple. "That will never do. I shall don a glittering dressing gown instead."

"I am sorry. But you cannot," Sarila said. "A cloth is what a new girl wears at her presentation."

I realized that I was behaving like a princess and not a slave, but I was worried about my appearance. I had far too much at stake to leave my beauty to chance. "What color of cloth?"

"There is no standard."

"Then I would like a brilliant shade of blue." A color that I thought suited me. "Can we do something extra special to make me stand out?"

"Besides the mask?" Sarila mixed my hair dye.

I stepped into the water. "I do not think the master was impressed with the notion of a mask."

Sarila responded, "He will be once he sees how mysterious it makes you look. But we can certainly do something extra special."

"We can bejewel your breasts," Ruby suggested. "To complement your navel gem."

I leaned back in the tub. "That should do nicely. Baki told the master that Afyon was creative." Once again, my anxiety surfaced. "I am afraid," I admitted softly.

"So was I," Sarila told me. "My knees trembled at my presentation. I was worried that the master would not like me as well as his other girls. Or that he would reject me altogether."

I studied her features. It was obvious that she was from a nearby region. "How did you become a slave?"

"I was captured and sold to a trader when the village where I lived was raided. My family was killed. I am alone now, except for my harem sisters."

I was tempted to touch her hand, to comfort her, but I did not know how to be a sister, harem or otherwise. I had been born an only child—a lonely princess dreaming of her prince.

Mired in emotion, I turned to Ruby. "What incited your capture?"

"Mine was similar to what we fabricated for you. I was on

my way to the colonies to become an indentured servant. A lowly maid." She flashed an impish smile. "Being a harem girl is far nicer than making beds and emptying chamber pots."

Sarila returned Ruby's smile, but I was unsure how to react. Once again, I was at a loss. I had never made a bed or emptied a chamber pot.

After my hair was dyed, dried and luxuriously styled, the girls went to work on my disguise, creating an exquisite blue mask with painted quail feathers, sapphires and fancy trim to offset the simple wrap I was to wear. They applied tiny sapphires around my areolas, too, calling attention to my generously rouged nipples.

From there, I practiced my French, perfecting the lilting accent Baki had boasted about to the master.

I also practiced kneeling on a carpet, with my face to the floor, while holding the cloth closed in an elegant manner.

Baki played along, ordering me to stand and disrobe, as if he were the master. As my heart began to pound, I wondered how I was going to fare when the real moment arrived.

"You hesitated," the eunuch said.

"I am new at this," I snapped back.

He made a worried expression. "Is that how you intend to speak to the master?"

"No, of course not."

I returned to my knees and we practiced again and again. I was determined to get it right, and just when I thought I was striking a sensual pose, one of the sapphires around my nipples popped off. Ruby giggled first, and then Sarila joined her. Even Baki chuckled.

I tried to maintain my decorum, then, realizing how foolish I looked, I laughed, too. But soon the jewel was reapplied and I continued my quest.

Until it was time to face the master.

～

Baki escorted me to David's apartment, but rather than enter through the bedchamber door, I was taken to his private dining area.

He was seated at a table with remnants of his meal left over. Although my head was lowered, I was stealing glances at him through my lashes, trying to see him through the eyes of a harem girl.

He was magnificent, handsome and virile and intimidating. He had the same effect on me as his wife, too. Either way, I was in a state of anxious flutter.

As Baki brought me farther into the room, David shifted his legs and angled his body toward us, all the while sipping a cup of tea.

So relaxed, so casual. I envied him that.

Once I was close enough to pay him respect, I dropped to my knees and clutched the cloth, holding it softly against my nakedness.

I kept my face pressed to the carpet, and from my vantage point, I could see David's sandaled feet and the rings on his toes.

He continued to savor his tea. I could hear him pouring another cup and stirring sugar into it.

"So this is Afyon," he said to Baki.

"Yes, Your Highness."

"How much training did you say she had?"

"None. She is still unschooled in the ways of pleasuring a master."

"But she has perfected our language?"

"She was on her way to be a tutor in the colonies when she was captured. Book work comes easily to her."

"A slave who can read and write." David clanked his spoon. "Interesting."

As they spoke, as they rehashed everything that Baki had told David earlier, my anxiety worsened. Was the master doing this purposefully? Making me wait while they talked about me? Already I was beginning to tremble.

I worried, too, that if I was kept in this position much longer, my knees would have unbecoming marks from the carpet, and I would fail to make an elegant presentation.

Finally he said, "Stand and show yourself to me."

Immediately, I reacted. Rising to his command, I removed my wrap and allowed it to slide luxuriously to the floor. I kept my gaze lowered, but I could feel him staring at me. His pe-

rusal made my skin warm and my nipples hard. I prayed that none of my sapphires came loose.

"Look at me," he said.

I lifted my gaze to meet his, and my heart nearly beat its way out of my bejeweled chest.

As our gazes locked, I feared that he would know me. That somehow, he would see his wife.

He came closer and reached out to trace the length of a feather on my mask. I breathed a little easier. From what I could tell, there was no recognition in his eyes.

"So, you wish to serve me?" he said.

"Yes, Master." I spoke in his language, but I gave him a taste of my feigned accent.

He thumbed one of my nipples, making it harder than it already was. He then skimmed my stomach, causing an eruption of butterflies. When he came to my pubis, I was so nervous, so strangely aroused, I made a soft sound.

He pressed two fingers against the top of my mound, directly above my cleft. "You should have worn a jewel here, too."

"Next time I will," I promised.

"Did I say there was going to be a next time?"

Instantly aware of my blunder, I dropped my chin, trying to appear humbled and hoping I had not taken my eagerness too far.

I could not look to Baki for guidance. The eunuch was standing behind me.

David gave me an order. "*Turn around. I want to see the other side of you.*"

I did his bidding, then remained motionless while he examined my backside. He ran a hand down my spine, all the way to my bottom.

I was finally able to exchange a glance with Baki, but he did not react. He was waiting for David to decide if I was worthy of the harem. I was waiting, too.

"*Turn back around,*" *David said.*

I ceased looking at Baki and faced the master. Silence passed between us, and I feared that he was going to reject me on the spot.

"*You are a widow?*" *he asked.*

"*Yes.*"

"*Then you must be aware of what pleases a man.*"

"*Somewhat,*" *I told him, hoping it was the right thing to say and wishing that I was still a virgin. Of course, if I was untouched, then I would not be his wife. Nor would I be desperate to seduce him. My wish made no sense.*

"*Surely you must have performed oral pleasure on your husband.*" *He put a finger to my lips and traced the shape of them, but his touch did not linger. He seemed cautious about being too affectionate.*

"*I . . .*"

"*You what? Speak up.*"

"*I did not pleasure my husband in that way.*"

"Why not?"

Yes, why not? I thought, scrambling for a logical response.

"I was a newlywed," I finally said. It was the only thing I could think of, and for the most part it was true. "Our intimacy had been limited to a small number of times."

David then asked, "Was he murdered by pirates when you were captured?"

His prolonged interest in my husband heightened my discomfort, but I responded quickly. "No, he did not lose his life on the ship. It was the year prior. He took ill soon after our nuptials." I decided that my grieving period should be over, otherwise my eagerness to become a harem girl might seem unnatural.

David looked past me at Baki. "Who do you think is best suited to be her instructor?"

The eunuch responded, "Since she has already formed a bond with Sarila and Ruby, I would choose them."

"Two instructors?"

"It would expedite her training."

David went quiet, but he seemed to be mulling it over. I scarcely breathed. I assumed that he was considering keeping me. Why else would my instruction matter?

He told Baki, "Send Sarila and Ruby to my bedchamber tonight." He paused to look at me. "And send Afyon with them. She can watch her instructors pleasure me."

"Yes, Your Highness," the eunuch responded, as I went weak inside.

David was obviously keeping me. But in the process, I would be witnessing him with the women who were supposed to be helping me win his favor.

It was not a scenario I would have chosen.

CHAPTER EIGHT

On Sunday, Beverly waited around to see if Jay would call. To make arrangements for the sundae, she thought.

Was she losing her mind? Wanting to have sex with food as the subject, and with her ex-husband, no less?

The phone rang, and she nearly jumped out of her skin. She checked the screen, and it said unknown caller. Was Jay using a blocked number?

"Hello?" she answered anxiously.

A male telemarketer came on the line, asking her to participate in an ice-cream survey.

Was this part of her seduction?

It didn't sound like Jay, but he was an actor and good with voices. Regardless, she wasn't about to say something in case it wasn't him. But she agreed to answer the questions.

He asked, "What's your favorite ice-cream flavor?"

She thought for a minute and said, "Chocolate chip cookie dough."

"And your favorite topping sauce?"

"I like all kinds. Chocolate, caramel, strawberry. That marshmallow stuff is good, too."

"Do you prefer sundaes or banana splits?"

Okay, now she totally wondered if he was Jay. She even got fluttery thinking that it could be him. But still, his voice seemed too plain, too generic. There was nothing sexual in his tone.

"Ma'am?" he said. "Are you still there?"

"What? Oh, yes. I prefer sundaes."

"Whipped cream?"

"Yes."

"Cherries?"

"Yes."

"Nuts?"

She stalled again, recalling how Jay had bumped her with his balls when they'd talked about nuts. "Just two."

"Two?" He sounded confused. "Two different kinds you mean?"

"Yes," she said, unable to explain. If he wasn't Jay, she would feel the total fool.

"What about candy sprinkles?"

"I like those, too."

When the conversation turned to brands of ice cream, she started thinking that this really was a legitimate survey.

It droned on and on, and Beverly blew out a sigh. Finally, the telemarketer thanked her and it was over.

Damn, she thought. *Damn.*

She hung up and frowned at the receiver. She could call Jay, she supposed, but she dreaded being in the weaker position. She wanted him to pursue her.

Had he lost interest? She hadn't heard from him since they'd agreed to have an affair. But that was only yesterday at breakfast. She almost laughed, thinking how impatient she was. Nonetheless, she paced the apartment.

About an hour later, her doorbell sounded. She made a mad dash, hoping, hoping . . .

She flung open the door, and there was Jay with a cheeky grin on his face. He held up a reusable shopping bag and said, "Sunday sundae."

She was too excited not to show it. "Get in here." She grabbed his arm and pulled him inside. "Let me see what you bought."

"Sure thing." He stepped back and let her empty the bag.

As soon as Beverly removed a carton of chocolate chip cookie dough ice cream she knew the guy on the phone had been him.

"*You.*" She pointed an accusatory finger.

"Two nuts?" he said in the generic voice and started to laugh.

She swatted his shoulder and continued removing items from the bag. He'd purchased everything she claimed to like: caramel, chocolate and strawberry sauces, marshmallow topping, whipped cream, maraschino cherries, and candy sprinkles.

"I have a shower curtain liner out in the car," he said.

She glanced up. "What?"

"To cover the bed. Unless you don't mind getting this stuff all over your sheets."

"No. The shower curtain liner is a good idea."

"That's what I figured you'd say. I'll be right back."

"Okay." What a strange experience, she thought. What an odd thrill.

While he went out to the car, she repacked the sundae ingredients and carried them into the bedroom, along with some serving spoons.

Jay returned and joined her by the bed. The liner he'd purchased was hot pink.

"Interesting choice," she said.

"I didn't want one of those boring old white ones. Besides, Pink is sort of my nickname."

"Like the singer? She's a girl, Jay."

"No, no, not like her. Pink was the color of the boutonniere I wore on my lapel during a masquerade ball. Luke and I were made up to look exactly the same, except his rose was red, and mine was pink. So he became known as Red that night, and I got stuck with Pink." He tore open the liner. "Lucky me, huh?"

"Apparently you learned to own it." She angled her head. "Where was this ball?"

"In New Mexico at an estate that belongs to Amber's family. It was the first time we had a ménage. It's the night that started it all." He added, "Luke's been giving Amber red roses ever since."

"And you brought me a pink shower curtain liner."

He spread it over the bed. "I thought about bringing you a rose, too. But I didn't want it to seem like I was courting you or trying to make more out of our affair than it is."

"That's fine." She wasn't about to admit that she would have appreciated a flower. "We're supposed to keep it simple."

"And sexy." He smiled. "Take off your clothes, baby. It's time to make a sundae."

She removed her top. "I can't believe we're doing this."

"I think there's a word for it."

"What? *Crazy?*"

"No." He laughed a little. "A word for the fetish of eating food off of someone's body. I guess we could check the Internet."

"I think I'd prefer not to know." She wasn't keen on considering herself as having sexual fetishes. But as she peeled off her jeans, preparing to become Jay's dessert, she couldn't deny that she was desperate for the gooey feel of it.

After discarding her bra and panties, she climbed onto the hot pink liner. It was slick and exciting. She'd never bedded down on vinyl before. She wasn't sure if she should spread her legs or keep them together, so she parted them slightly, going for an in-between position.

Jay cleared a nightstand and placed all of the ingredients on it. He got a stack of towels from the bathroom, too. Organized, she thought.

"Want to sample the ice cream?" He dipped into the carton with a serving spoon and held it out.

She tasted the treat from the oversized utensil and the bigness of it almost seemed phallic.

"Good?" he asked.

She nodded, swallowed. It was wonderfully sweet.

He offered her another bite, then quickly kissed the ice cream from her lips, making her moan for more of the same.

He gave her what she wanted, feeding her again. This time he waited until the ice cream was inside her mouth before he kissed her. The sensation made her tighten her toes. Lord, he was hot. And the ice cream was cold.

The next spoonful was placed on her stomach, and she shivered. But she watched, too, fascinated by the way he'd begun building the sundae.

He added another scoop, and she kept still. Next, he

opened the sauces and poured the chocolate on first, swirling it in a circular pattern. After that came the strawberry, then caramel. Beverly was getting good and sticky. But there was more to come.

So much more.

Jay stuck a spoon into the Marshmallow Fluff and placed a glob onto the burgeoning sundae.

When he popped the lid on the whipped cream can, her breath whooshed out. He looked like a gunslinger with an itchy trigger finger.

Beverly shouldn't have told the telemarketer that she liked so many toppings. But he was the one who was going to have to eat the lovely mess he was making.

He created whipped cream rosettes, sprinkled the candy, and placed two cherries on top.

By now, the ice cream was melting against the warmth of her skin and dripping in all directions. She watched a rivulet run along her inner thigh. Jay watched it, too, then looked up to meet her gaze.

He said, "You look yummy," then removed his T-shirt and tossed it aside.

In the next lust-crazed instant, he dived in with his hands and spread the sundae all over her naked body, concentrating mainly on her breasts and the V between her thighs.

"Tell me what it feels like," he said.

She grabbled for words to describe it. One of the cherries

was dangerously close to her nether lips, adhering to a stream of marshmallow and whipped cream.

"Wild," she finally said. "Wet. Messy."

"Lick your nipples, Bev, and let me watch."

Now it made sense as to why he'd created the sundae to her specifications. He wanted her to participate, too.

Since her breasts were big enough to make the grade, she easily grabbed one and lifted it toward her mouth. As instructed, she flicked her tongue over her nipple. Instantly, she tasted an explosion of flavors, and she moaned from the carnality of it.

"You'd better make me come," she told him.

"I will." But at the moment, he was fixated on what she was doing. "Do that to the other one."

Beverly wasn't about to deny him. She liked the way he was looking at her. She knew of clubs that allowed their dancers to perform specialty acts, like dousing themselves in chocolate syrup on stage, and now she knew why.

She tasted her other nipple, and Jay went down on her, licking the gooiness between her legs.

Sweet heaven.

She bent her knees so she could watch through the opening. The plastic creaked, making a Slip 'n Slide sound, like the game she used to play as a child.

When he took the nearby cherry and put it inside of her, she gasped. "What you are doing?"

"Making you a virgin again."

"That's not funny."

"Who's being funny?"

"You can't pop a cherry that's already been popped."

"Wanna bet?" He pushed it in a little deeper, but not so far that he wouldn't be able to reach it later with his tongue.

"You're nasty, Jay." And she was losing her dirty little mind because she liked it. She even lifted her pelvis, making his job easier.

He went down on her again, taking long, teasing licks. Beverly ran her hands along her body, caressing her own skin. She had goop all over, but somehow it seemed magical. Amid the foreplay mess, the candy sprinkles shimmered.

Finally Jay went after the cherry, sucking it into his mouth. She imagined how it tasted, mingled with the flavor of a woman.

Encouraging him to play some more, she searched for the other cherry, which had fallen to the vinyl covering. Beyond sanity, she picked it up and handed it to him.

He took it, but he didn't put it inside her. Instead, he rolled it over her clit, making little circles.

Without a doubt, she was losing her mind. She wanted him to give her the cherry when he was done.

He looked up, and they stared at each other. She continued rubbing her sundae-smeared skin, and the sensation of caressing herself while he played with her pussy was more than she could bear.

The climax started at her clit and worked its way through nerve endings she didn't know she had. She closed her eyes and lost sight of Jay. But she could still feel him, *there*, at her most sensitive spot.

Beverly gave up the fight and arched her back, letting the convulsions take over.

She shook and shook, then became aware of Jay moving forward. She opened her eyes to find him leaning over her, holding the cherry. He squeezed the preserved fruit and made its juice drip onto her lips. He almost seemed like a vampire, giving her his blood.

As another climax burst through her body, he kissed her, hard and deep, thrusting his tongue. She clutched his shoulders, imprinting him with even more of the sticky sweetness that rubbed between them.

After it was over and the sexual dizziness passed, he fed her the cherry for her final reward, leaving her deliciously spent.

"God help me," she said.

"Yeah, me, too."

Now that her vision had cleared, she realized that he was still wearing his jeans, which were coated in gunk and tented with a hard-on.

"Poor baby." She cupped his fly, feeling him up through the denim. "He didn't get his."

He pushed back against the sticky pressure. "No, but he plans to."

"Not right now, I hope." She couldn't imagine getting laid like this.

"In the shower." He sat up and grabbed two towels from the nightstand. "But first we need to clean up a bit."

Not only did they wipe themselves down, they sopped up the liner to keep it from dripping onto the floor and got rid of it. Jay cleared the nightstand, too, putting the sundae fixings away.

By the time they were ready for the shower, the evidence of their food play was gone, and he was armed with a condom in his hand. He set it on the side of the tub, and they took turns lathering their bodies and washing their hair.

While steam gathered, he leaned forward, and soon she was pinned against the tiled wall, his nakedness pressed against hers.

They kissed, hot and rough and sloppy, like teenagers learning to French. Water dripped from their foreheads and trailed down their faces, trickling into their mouths.

Beverly wondered what losing her virginity to him would have been like. Clearly, the cherry-popping thing was still fresh in her mind.

She pondered it on another level. If Jay had been David in her last life, then, in a sense, she actually had lost her virginity to him. Unfortunately it hadn't gone so well that time. But there was no way to know, short of Jay being regressed himself, if he and David were the same man.

He ended the kiss and reached for the condom. He didn't seem like a teenager anymore. He seemed strong and confident and domineering.

He sheathed himself and ordered her to turn around. Eager for his penetration, she faced the wall.

He moved her hair out the way so he could nibble at her nape. Stallion-style bites. Hungry shivers.

He steadied his hands on her hips, angling her. She felt his penis probing her labia and seeking entrance.

"Did you know that there's a scented product called Vulva?" he asked. "It's sold in little vials and smells like a woman."

"That's weird, Jay."

"I think it's sexy. Animalistic."

All right, so maybe he had a point, especially since the olfactory senses were often involved in feral mating practices.

"Sexy in a weird way," she said. Feral or not, she couldn't quite fathom a product that mimicked the scent of a woman. "Honestly, who would wear it?"

"Someone who wants to get themselves off. Me? I'd sniff it right from the vial."

He slid into her, and inch by inch, she took him. On a groan, he shafted deeper. She suspected that he was thinking about the mystery of a woman's vulva—the secret place that inspired a fragrance of fuck-me pheromones.

He grabbed a hold of her hair and tugged her face to the side so they could battle for a kiss.

She tried not to consider how long their affair would last. Or wouldn't last. For now she was consumed with him, as he was with her.

He moved in and out, and she imagined his glutes tightening with each thrusting motion. The athleticism of his body had always made her wet.

She was wet now, her juices stirring. The sound of the shower pummeling the tub and splashing down the drain added to the ambience. So did the rising steam. It got thicker and thicker.

Jay pumped harder, his balls slapping against her butt. When he bit her neck again, her pulse thudded beneath his teeth. So many sensations.

"Touch yourself," he told her.

She slid a hand to her clit.

He said, "Now taste it."

She brought her fingers to her lips and licked. He watched from over her shoulder.

"Do it from inside."

"You're inside me."

"Then touch and taste us both."

She maneuvered her hand to cop a feel, and cream welled from her sex. The mouthful she got was warm and sticky.

He rasped against her ear. "Give me some."

She dipped in and reached back to feed him. He sucked the juice from her fingers and made a rough sound. She tried to forget that they'd once been married, but he held her hips in a death grip, claiming her in the way only an ex-husband could.

Painful. Possessive.

She knew he was about to pop. But so was she. She didn't want to come at the same time. Not with him holding her so tightly. But she couldn't control her lust, and she certainly couldn't control his.

There was no escape.

They climaxed as one, hot and raging and primal. She shook and shivered, then sagged against the wall.

He pulled out and dropped his head against her shoulder, breathing heavily. She reminded herself that this was just sex, a reminder that didn't make a hill of beans after the fact.

"You should get back on birth control," he said. "Like before."

She frowned at the wall. *Like before* meant when they were a genuine couple. "Why? So you can come without a condom?"

"Just think how wet you'd be." He laughed and nipped her ear. "Your juice and my jism."

She turned around to look at him. "You're the worst."

He grinned. "For making you want to laugh?"

She nodded and burst into a ridiculous chuckle. Their conversation had started with pussy perfume.

"We're good together, Bev."

"Good at sex," she agreed.

"And good humor. How many other exes could do this?"

Not many, she thought. "Maybe we're just crazy."

"Maybe we are." He got rid of the condom and turned off the water.

They stepped out of the tub and used the last of the clean towels. He slicked his damp hair back, and she marveled at how handsome he was. He seemed to be marveling at her, too.

"Will you go to a party with me?" he asked.

Caught off guard, she started. "When and where?"

"It's the Saturday after next. In Santa Fe."

"New Mexico?" The place where his first ménage occurred? "Does this party have something to do with Luke and Amber?"

"It's to celebrate their engagement. Ethan Tierney is hosting it. He's an artist and a friend of Amber's. He paints BDSM depictions."

She blinked. "Bondage and discipline and all that?"

"Yeah. He's into that lifestyle. He's rich as sin, too. It's going to be a major shindig."

"You want me to drive to New Mexico with you for a kinky party?"

"We'd be flying, and who said it was kinky?"

"So it's not?"

Jay wrapped the towel he'd used around his waist. "There

will be wild things going on in the dungeons if anyone wants to watch. But we don't have to watch if you don't want to."

She covered up, too. She wasn't sure how she felt about sex dungeons or voyeurism or meeting his ménage partners for that matter. "Are they into bondage?"

"Who?"

"Luke and Amber?"

"No. But they're open-minded about other people's fetishes. Besides, it's a masquerade party, and they're totally into that. All of the men are supposed to dress like grooms, and all of the women are supposed to be costumed as brides."

The plot thickens, she thought. And it made her even more nervous. "I'm already a bride at work."

"You can wear a different costume at the party. In fact, I was thinking that we could pattern ourselves after David and Camille. We could dress similar to them on their wedding day. But with masks. Or maybe you could be more of a harem bride. And I could be your husband and your master." He shrugged, smiled. "It would go with the bondage theme. Besides, that sounds sexy, don't you think?"

Sexy and strange, she thought.

Jay didn't know that Camille had disguised herself to infiltrate the harem or that her husband had become her master.

"What?" he asked, apparently noticing her expression.

Without further hesitation, she proceeded to tell him about Camille's foray into David's erotic world.

He listened, quite obviously intrigued. "So not only was she a princess, she was a harem girl, too. How lucky could David be?"

"Lucky enough. The first time Afyon was summoned to his bedchamber was to watch him with the girls who were instructing her."

"Dang. That's kind of like us watching a threesome at the party. But more so. That David was quite a guy."

Yes, she thought, quite a guy. And she couldn't help but wonder, for the umpteenth time, if Jay *was* David.

CHAPTER NINE

I was more nervous than I imagined possible. Sarila and Ruby help me get ready, but they readied themselves, too, flitting about the dressing room.

Palpable excitement thickened the air, with other harem girls rushing this way and that, fussing over the three of us. Someone suggested that we don similar costumes, but in different colors, and that was how we were attired.

Each of us sported sheer tops and hazy skirts, so our nakedness could be seen beneath the fabrics. Mine was blue to complement my mask, where even more feathers and adornments had been added. The extra sapphire the master had requested shimmered against my pubis, and the rest glittered in unison around my areolas. To accentuate the henna in my hair, I wore a variety of jeweled combs and tasseled ornaments.

Ruby's costume was a rich emerald green, a color that enhanced her fair skin and glorious red hair. Gold hoops graced her pierced nipples. She wore a gold cosmetic on her eyelids, too. In fact, her entire body shimmered from a gilded powder she had used.

Sarila had chosen to elongate her eyes with black kohl, giving her the seductive look of an Egyptian queen. Her alluring costume was a pale shade of yellow, and she wore ankle bells and jangling bracelets that made delicate music whenever she moved.

We made a fetching trio. But that was the point. Baki warned us not to compete with each other. Our purpose was to entice the master equally.

As was the usual harem practice, we wore flavored honey between our legs in case David decided to taste us there. That, of course, would be his choice when the time came. Mostly we had been summoned so that Ruby and Sarila could perform oral pleasure on him and so that I could watch and learn.

Baki approached me. "Remember to kneel on the runner that leads to the master's bed and crawl toward him when he commands you."

I wrung my hands together. "I will."

He made a troubled face. "You need to quell your anxiety."

I lowered my hands, trying to appear calm, but the butter-flies in my stomach told an internal tale.

Just then, a bell sounded from outside the harem walls, heightening my nervousness. I knew it was David pulling the green cord beside his bed.

Ruby and Sarila rushed over to me, aware that the master was ready for the evening to begin.

Baki escorted us to our destination and swiftly departed.

David waited for us in bed, dressed only in a pair of light-weight pants. Leaning against an array of cushions, he looked wildly handsome and typically confident.

Seeing him there reminded me of our debauched wedding night, and I wished that I had him all to myself to make up for it. But I supposed in some ways it was easier being in the com-pany of my instructors. At least I could follow their lead.

We got on our knees and crawled along the runner toward him. Sarila's jewelry jangled, adding sultry sounds to our advancement.

We stopped at the foot of his bed and waited for his com-mand. My heart pounded in my chest.

"Rise," he said.

Simultaneously, we stood, and he looked us over in that lordly manner of his. His perusal made my skin tingle.

He motioned to Sarila and Ruby. "You may join me." He gestured to me. "You, Afyon, shall wait there."

My companions moved forward and climbed into bed with

my husband. When they glanced back at me, I could tell they were concerned about why the master had not invited me to come closer.

I was concerned, too. Was it his intention to have me watch from a distance? To stand off by myself until they were done?

David told both girls to remove their tops, and the play-time began. As he encouraged Ruby to rub her pierced nipples against him, he leaned toward Sarila and slid his hand up her skirt and along her thigh and toward her center. She moaned and spread her legs.

He slipped a finger into her damp folds, and she lifted her hips to accommodate him.

Continuing his quest, he thrust yet another finger into her. I struggled with a sense of envy, of arousal, of confusion. I wanted him to be touching me.

He withdrew his fingers and tasted them. I knew that Sarila had chosen mint-flavored honey to sweeten herself, whereas I had picked an apricot blend. I widened my stance and realized that I was getting moist down there.

The master turned toward Ruby, putting his fingers into her. She lifted her skirt all the way up and exposed herself while he stroked her.

She and Sarila seemed so fluid, so natural in everything they did. I worried that I would never be as sensual as they were.

David tasted the honey from Ruby, and after partaking of

her flavor, which I knew to be pomegranate, he sat forward and shifted his attention to me.

He snared me with his dark gaze, and I stared back at him, grateful for the emotional shield my mask provided.

"You do it," he said. "To yourself."

Determined to prove my worth, I refused to falter. Still, I wondered how to touch and taste myself in an imaginative way. If I lifted my skirt, I would look as if I were mimicking Ruby, and if I slid my hand under it, I would be copying what David had done to Sarila.

So I lowered my skirt and stepped out of it as provocatively as I could. I removed my top, as well, discarding it with wanton abandon. I was now completely naked while the other women remained half clothed. Even the master still wore his pants, although he was visibly hard beneath them.

With my heart beating a fiery rhythm, I rubbed my hands all over my body. I circled the jewels that decorated my nipples, then worked my way down to the sapphire that shimmered at my mound.

David watched every move I made. Ruby and Sarila watched, too. I felt downright scandalous.

I finally reached between my legs and inserted a finger. I was soft and warm and tight. But moist and sticky, too.

I inserted another finger, then pressed both of them against my tongue and licked the feminine sweetness. David reacted by freeing his erection and encouraging Sarila and Ruby to pleasure him.

Eagerly sharing their master, they took turns. Back and forth they went, taking him into their mouths. They moved their hands up and down, too, creating an even deeper motion.

He opened his legs so I could view their luscious services. But he also motioned for me to touch and taste myself again, to give him a repeat performance while he savored the hands and mouths that spoiled him.

I responded to his carnal persuasion and did what was expected of me. Yet I envied the other girls for being so close to him. While Sarila pleasured him, her jewelry chimed in naughty merriment.

He tangled his hands in her hair, treating her with rugged affection. Ruby garnered his affection, too. He tugged her toward his face and kissed her. I saw their tongues meet and mate in the French way.

I quit touching myself. Instead, I simply stood naked in my husband's bedchamber and watched him enjoy his lewd encounter.

Part of me was aroused and another part was appalled that I had put myself in this situation. Was it worth the ache? At the moment, I was not sure.

I studied Sarila and the way her cheeks hollowed. Clearly, she was taking David all the way to the back of her throat.

Would I ever be able to take him that deeply?

He continued to kiss Ruby, and the exchange got rougher. He twisted the rings in her nipples, and she moaned in a blend of passion and pain.

From there, he lowered both hands to the top of Sarila's head and held her firmly in place. He also raised his hips and thrust forward, increasing the tempo.

He finally ended the kiss with Ruby, but she knew enough not to remain idle. She got behind David and pressed herself against him, nibbling his shoulders and sliding her hands down to caress his chest.

What a wildly companionable trio they made: the master sitting forward with his legs wide open, Ruby nuzzling behind him, and Sarila with her head in his lap.

Once again, David looked directly at me, and I gazed back at him. Afyon, the slave I had become, was supposed to be watching and learning, and she was. But Camille, the wife in disguise, remained trapped in emotion.

This was my husband's world, the lifestyle in which he had been raised, and the bond he shared with his other women could not be denied.

As his breathing quickened, he tipped his head back and leaned against Ruby. I watched intently, aware that he was on the threshold of orgasm.

His body tensed, and I gauged the tautness of his features. He tightened his hold on Sarila, gripping her even harder than before.

All of his reactions seemed instinctual except for the fact that his eyes were open. That was not natural, I thought. I sensed that he wanted to close them, yet in spite of the sluggish angle of his head, he seemed determined to hold my gaze, making certain I continued to watch.

To combat the undeniable heat that sizzled through me, I touched my pubis the way I had done earlier. But it was not enough. I desperately wanted to be close to David, to please him, so I moved forward and offered him my fingers, pressing them against his lips.

He tasted my honey and began to shudder. Within seconds, a feral sound rumbled from his chest, and he climaxed hard and fast, spurting into Sarila's mouth.

She swallowed without spilling a drop.

Afterward, she waited for Ruby to join her, where they rested their heads against David's thighs. He rewarded them by petting their hair. I almost expected them to purr like pampered kittens.

Now that my part in it was over, I did not know what to do. He was looking at me in a displeased way.

"Did I tell you to place your fingers against my mouth?" he asked.

"No," I said, confused that he was chastising me when he had gotten excited by what I had done. "But I thought it would please you."

A breath of silence passed before he said, "An untrained slave does not decide what is best for her master."

"*I understand,*" *I told him, dropping down to issue an apology.*

Being on my knees put me closer to Ruby and Sarila. Both exchanged disappointed glances with me.

Afyon was not faring as well as we had hoped. David motioned for me to rise, and I came to my feet once again.

"*Get dressed,*" *he told me.*

As I put on my clothes, Ruby and Sarila were instructed to remove the rest of theirs and curl up in bed, where they would remain with my husband.

As for me, Baki was summoned.

Once the eunuch arrived, David said to him, "Afyon is too impulsive and needs to learn her place. Keep her in the harem until she is properly trained."

"*As you wish.*" *Although Baki treated the master with respect, he also managed to come to my defense. "But please take pity on her, Your Highness. She cannot help how eager she is to serve you."*

David did not respond, but he did turn to look at me.

As we gazed at each other, we fell into a strange sort of hush. My heart skittered the entire time. Everyone else remained quiet, too. Even Sarila's jewelry was silent.

Finally, he broke eye contact and addressed Baki by changing the subject. "You may retrieve Ruby and Sarila at first light. Also, inform my wife that I will be joining her for breakfast. In her apartment, so make certain those arrangements are made."

The eunuch agreed without batting an eye, but once we left the master's bedchamber, he seemed worried. As we walked down the corridor toward the harem courtyard, he blew out a hasty breath.

"His Highness sent you away, but he wants to see his wife? What do you think that means?"

"I have no idea," I responded, just as fretful. With David it was difficult to tell. My husband was not a predictable man.

～

I awakened early, and now I was dressed and waiting, all remnants of last night's masquerade gone. No jewels, no colorful kohl around my eyes, no feathers, no henna-tinged hair. I was Princess Camille once again.

I still could not fathom why David wanted to see me, but I was anxious to find out.

He arrived in his riding attire, obviously intending to visit the stables after breakfast.

"Good morning," he said, sounding quite proper.

I bade him the same greeting, and we proceeded to my private dining area and sat across from each other at a small but elegant table.

Our tea was served, along with boiled eggs, flatbread, olives and cheese. Cups of diced apricots, smothered in cream and garnished with sugar and walnuts, were presented, as well.

David waved the servants away so we could dine alone.

139

After they departed, he reached for his fruit cup. I started with the eggs. The apricots reminded me of the honey I had worn between my legs, as it was the flavor I'd chosen. It also reminded me of the mistake I had made.

While David spooned the creamy concoction into his mouth, I studied him. Had he requested apricots or was it coincidence that they had been prepared for this particular day?

Before silence befell us, I garnered the courage to ask, "What brings you to my table this morning?"

He swallowed the food. "Does a husband need a reason to dine with his wife?"

"He does if the husband is you, and the wife is me."

I expected him to lift those condescending brows, but instead he managed a rare smile. Apparently my remark amused him.

"Well?" I asked, pressing him for an answer and struggling with his effect on me. His smile actually seemed a tad boyish, making me sweetly aware of my childhood dreams.

"I thought you might be interested in Afyon's progress," he said.

My heart leaped directly to my throat, and I forced out a breath. "Your new harem girl? Why would I concern myself with her?"

"Considering how nosy you were about her yesterday, I assumed you would be curious."

I was not going to deny myself the benefit of this conversa-

tion. *"Maybe I am a little curious."* For strong measure, I sent him a wifely glare. *"Did you bed her already?"*

"No, but I allowed her to watch."

Instantly, my body temperature rose. I sipped my tea, wetting my lips and wishing I had a cool beverage instead.

"Watch what?" I dared to ask.

"How to give oral pleasure. She witnessed me being tended by two girls."

"And which two might that be?" I asked, pretending that I was unaware.

"Ruby and Sarila. Baki chose them as her instructors."

I frowned, allowing him to believe that I disapproved. *"Is that typical of how a new girl is trained?"*

"Normally she would receive weeks of instruction before she entered my bedchamber."

"Then why did you allow her the privilege of special training?"

He finished his apricots, savoring the last bite, conjuring an image of how readily he had tasted my fingers last night and how powerfully he had climaxed.

"When I first saw her, she intrigued me," he said.

My heart dipped and dived. I busied myself with my eggs. *"Does she intrigue you still?"*

"I find her complicated."

I tried to behave with indifference. *"What does that mean?"*

"*She reminds me of you, Camille.*"

I struggled to keep my wits. Did he suspect me? Had he arranged this discussion to gauge my reaction?

Searching for the right response, I asked, "In what manner do you find us similar?"

David spread cheese on his bread. "The way in which she carries herself lends familiarity. Actually, her entire body is comparable to yours."

I formed a ready answer. "Sarila resembles me, too. That is why Baki chose her to replace me on our wedding night."

"Afyon resembles you more."

"Then it must be her breeding. If my memory serves me correctly, she is French. My homeland has French origins. It stands to reason that we might possess some of the same physical qualities."

"I suppose. But her spirit rivals yours, too."

"Her spirit?" I feigned offense. "How can that be? She is a slave, and I am a princess."

"Yes, but she seems too independent to be a slave."

Fear clamored inside me. "Are you going to send her away?"

"No. But I am not going to allow her to bewitch me."

Was that what I had done to him last night? Was that why he had chastised me? Before he noticed how invested I was in his comment, I criticized Afyon. "She is probably dreadful under her mask."

"*Nonsense. Baki would never purchase a dreadful slave for me.*"

"*Masks can be deceiving.*"

"*Not in this instance. I can tell that she is beautiful. Magnificently so.*"

I snared his gaze in the way a jealous wife would, and he bit into his bread. He certainly did not seem like a man who had just uncovered his bride's deceptive ruse.

"*Are you anxious to summon her to your bedchamber again?*" *I asked, my fear lessening.*

"*I am anxious to see if proper training will curb her independence.*"

I proceeded, pushing him further. "*Maybe you secretly admire her independence.*"

"*That would be like saying I admire your insolence, Camille.*"

"*Maybe you do.*"

"*Never,*" *he snapped.* "*Now quit chattering and let me eat in silence.*"

I fell quiet. In spite of his claim, I suspected that he was becoming captivated by me because of my likeness to Afyon. But that did not ensure my victory.

At the moment he looked as if he wanted to banish me, right along with his new harem girl.

CHAPTER TEN

After breakfast, I rushed over to the harem to tell Baki about my conversation with David.

Although he seemed relieved, he remained concerned about my training. "Afyon must prove herself. She must be everything he desires."

"I think in some ways she already is. Or almost is," I amended.

"Good. Now come. Your instructors have been waiting for you."

Baki escorted me to Sarila's room, where she and Ruby were. After they greeted me, Sarila proceeded to recount last night's events, telling me what had occurred after I had left.

"We napped for a while," she said. "Then the master wanted

us to tend to him again. But this time Ruby did most of the pleasuring."

"He straddled my face," the redhead chimed.

My skin turned warm. "Is that one of his common preferences?"

"Sometimes. But he was not focused on me. His mind was on you."

My pulse jumped. "Me or Afyon?"

"Afyon. He questioned Sarila about her while he knelt over me. It aroused him to discuss her."

Overwhelmed, I turned to Sarila. "What sorts of questions did he ask?"

She spoke softly, enhancing David's words. "Mostly he wanted to talk about her appearance. He wanted to know if I thought she was sweet and lush and beautiful."

Ruby then remarked, "He was caressing my face and rubbing himself against my lips, but it was Afyon who consumed him." She spoke without envy or malice. "When he pushed into my mouth, I could tell that he was imagining her."

I was both elated and afraid. My husband was having fantasies about the mysterious character I was portraying—a girl who created as much excitement in him as she did frustration. My training was even more crucial now.

Baki seemed to be thinking the same thing. He motioned to Sarila, and she opened a trunk at the foot of her bed and removed a carefully wrapped object. Upon unveiling it, she transferred it to me.

My heart hit my chest. In my hand, I held a smooth and shiny phallus, skillfully carved of wood.

"It is called an olisbos," she said. "It is a substitute for an erect penis. A tool we use to learn how to give oral pleasure to the master. We have a lovely collection of them. That one is yours is to keep and to practice on."

I gazed at the device. It even had ball sacs. "What if it splinters in my mouth?"

"That will not happen. It has been polished to perfection. And it is the same length and girth as the master. All of our olisboses were fashioned after him."

Oh, goodness, I thought, grateful for the opportunity to learn yet nervous just the same.

Baki interjected, "Men often give them to their wives to prevent hysteria when they are away for long periods of time. That way the wife can insert it into herself."

"Hysteria?" I asked.

"A woman needs to have a penis inside her. Or else she goes mad."

I glanced at Ruby and Sarila and noticed that they suppressed smiles. Apparently they did not believe this to be true. Neither did I, but maybe we were wrong. Maybe that was why I craved my husband so desperately.

Baki departed, allowing Ruby and Sarila to instruct me.

Sarila began the lesson by lubricating the olisbos with oil derived from an edible plant so that I was better able to slide my hands and mouth along it.

"Lick the head," she said. "And pay special attention to the slit at the tip."

I swirled my tongue, teasing the wood as if it were my husband.

"Caress it this way." She showed me how the master liked to be stroked. "Fondle the sacs, too. But be gentle with them."

I complied, running my hands on the underside of the phallus and cupping the sacs with care, even if they were made of wood.

"Now wrap your mouth around it, but cover your teeth with your lips."

Once again, I followed her instruction.

"Be sure to look up at him while you are doing it."

I lifted my gaze, and she praised my naughty effort.

"Good. Now use your tongue again, licking while you suck. Keep stimulating him."

I did whatever she told me to do.

"A little more." She encouraged me to go deeper.

I managed rather well. To prove how naturally skilled I was, I went considerably lower.

And gagged.

Ruby giggled. Up until now, she had been silent. "That used to happen to me when I first learned, too."

I removed the phallus from my mouth. "So what should I do?" Gagging on the master's penis was not in Afyon's best interest.

"Go slowly," she advised. "Take a little bit at a time and work up to it."

I practiced until my jaw was sore, but I still failed to take the entire length.

Ruby suggested that I use my hands to make up the difference until I conquered it. If I conquered it, she added. Apparently not all of the girls could perform that deeply. In fact, not many could.

I was determined to be one of the privileged few, even if it meant making the olisbos my constant companion.

My next lesson was getting accustomed to the taste of the master's cream or at least something relatively similar. I was provided a small cup with the whites of an egg that had been liquefied with milk, then seasoned with salt and a sprinkling of sugar.

Sarila said, "Sometimes the consistency and amount varies, but a harem girl must swallow whatever the master gives her."

I nodded, recalling how gracefully she had managed David's seed.

I sipped sparingly from the cup. It was as unpleasant as I assumed it would be, but at least it slid easily down my throat. I made a horrible face and sipped again.

"Some of the girls who have tasted other men claim that the master is sweeter than most," Sarila said. "That is why we added sugar."

I thought about the glazed dates he had eaten on our wedding night, as well as the apricots he had devoured this morning. "Maybe it is because of the treats he favors."

She considered my comment. "Maybe so." She motioned for me to finish the drink. "We shall give you another cup soon. Then you may swallow all of it at once and imagine that the master is spilling into you."

Regardless of the taste, the notion excited me. Already I was envisioning myself with my head in David's lap. I pictured him kneeling over my face, too, reenacting what he had done to Ruby.

Would he pet my hair when it was over? Would he coddle me like a kitten? I wanted to know that feeling, too.

I brought the wooden phallus up to my mouth and proceeded to pleasure it again. Ruby and Sarila watched, proud, it seemed, of their eager student.

I sucked with vigor and finished with a sensual smile. I had taken a bit more this time, forging toward my goal. As promised, I was given another small cup of the master's mock cream. As I swallowed the full amount, I got aroused. I even licked my lips. Then I went back and laved the phallus, as if I were bathing David with my tongue.

"The master is going to love you," Ruby said.

I blinked through the haze. She was speaking of love in a sexual way, but I wanted my husband to love me in every way. I lowered the olisbos.

"Is something wrong?" she asked.

"No," I lied, even if my melancholy was evident.

Sarila interceded, frowning with concern. "Maybe you need to rest."

Rather than respond, I contemplated my plight. Could a man, especially one continuously spoiled by female attention, be seduced into love? Or was I destined to fail?

There was no answer, not at this time. But if I abandoned my quest, I would never know.

"I want to continue," I finally said, prepared to do anything that was required of me.

In search of winning David's heart.

Jay sat behind the wheel of his car, en route to a costume shop. He glanced over at Beverly. She didn't seem too keen about the upcoming party, but she'd agreed to be his date nonetheless.

"What do you think Camille would think of this?" he asked.

"Think about what?"

"Me dressing up like David, and you dressing like a harem bride."

"She would probably like it."

"Did she actually have to crawl on her knees and call him master?"

"Yep."

"Are you going to do that with me?"

She shot him a "get real" look.

He shrugged. "You can't blame a guy for trying."

She shook her head, and they both laughed. They'd always shared the same goofy sense of humor, and being with her here, like this, on their way to get costumes, made him feel like her husband again.

He quit laughing. His feelings were far from funny. The last thing he needed was to fall for her a second time.

"What made you decide to get regressed?" he asked, serious now.

"One of my dance students is a certified past life therapist, and she got me interested in it."

"So you're teaching her to strip, and she's helping you connect with your past life." He stopped at a red light. "What's it like?"

"The hypnosis? It starts with a discussion, then goes into the regression. Each session takes about an hour and a half." She waited a beat before she expounded. "Some people reconnect through their feelings, others hear sounds or conversations, and some just seem to know who they once were. But for me, it's visual, almost like a movie. Sometimes it involves my other senses, too, like touch, taste and smell."

He considered how defined her experience was. "So how does that work?"

"Mostly it's associated with Camille's reactions to David. If she's touching him or tasting him or inhaling the scent of skin, then so am I."

The light turned green and he proceeded through the intersection. "That's pretty damn intimate."

She blew out a breath. "You're not going to start with the jealousy thing again, are you?"

Jay frowned at the windshield. "I don't know. Maybe."

"There's nothing to be jealous of if you used to be him."

"There's no evidence that I was."

She studied him. He could feel her staring at his profile. Then she said, "Maybe you should get regressed. Maybe we should find out for sure. At least it'll stop us from assuming or guessing or wondering."

Easy for her to say. Jay was already battling his feelings for Beverly, and if David had fallen for Camille, then he would be forced to relive that, too. The flip side was not being David at all, and that seemed even worse.

"I'd rather just be your master at the party," he said, getting himself off the hook.

She didn't respond, and the conversation was dropped. Silent, they arrived at their destination.

He parked on the street, and they took the sidewalk and entered the building.

The front of the store was crammed with vintage clothes and accessories. There were costumed mannequins, too. But most of the stock was presented through catalogs.

A rental clerk approached them. She appeared to be in her early twenties with teased black hair and a nose ring. Her attire was a blend of Goth and rockabilly. Or Gothabilly, he supposed.

Jay explained what they were looking for: costumes that represented a Middle Eastern prince/groom and harem girl/bride.

Soon they were seated at a table, paging through catalogs, with Ms. Gothabilly as their guide.

They started with Jay's costume, which was under the heading of Arabian Prince. There were a lot of styles to choose from, some simple, some elaborate.

He glanced at Beverly, watching her expression as she turned each page. He was allowing her to make the decision for him, but nothing was catching her eye.

"What exactly did David wear at the wedding?" he asked.

She replied vividly. "A jeweled tunic with a round collar, loose-fitting pants and a coiled headdress."

"In what colors?"

"Everything was white. Except for the jewels. They were in a variety of colors."

The clerk cocked her head. "If you don't mind me prying, who's David?"

Beverly glanced at Jay, leaving him with the burden. He stalled, then decided that Gothabilly would probably think the truth was cool.

"He's the prince she used to be married to. In her past life," he added.

Sure enough she reacted with enthusiasm. "Oh, wow. That's awesome." She looked admirably at his ex. "I could see you married to a prince." She then shifted to Jay. "Are you him?"

Damn, he thought. That again. "I don't know. I haven't been regressed."

Gothabilly returned her attention to Beverly and asked what the hypnosis had been like, and Bev repeated what she'd told Jay in the car.

Fascinated, the clerk seemed even more eager to help them find the perfect costume. She reached for another catalog and checked the index. "What about this? We could apply jewels to the tunic and add a turban. We could fancy it up as much as you want."

Beverly smiled. "That will actually work." She described the pattern in which the jewels should be applied, and soon she was looking at accessories.

Jay sat back while sandals and toe rings—yes, toe rings—were chosen for him.

When the time came to choose Beverly's costume, the clerk asked, "Do you have anything specific in mind that you'd like to wear?"

Beverly responded, "Actually, I'd like a harem dancer costume, but with a wedding flair, so it'll work for the party. It should definitely be white."

Curious now, Jay interjected. "Why a dance costume?"

"Because I'm a dancer, and so was Camille."

"She danced for David?"

Beverly nodded. "But the first time it wasn't just for him. It was at a small celebration with other men in attendance."

Shit, Jay thought. "She danced for other guys?"

"That's what David wanted her to do. To perform for all of them. To undress, too."

"Then I'm sure as hell not David," he said, annoyed that His Holy-Ass Highness had encouraged his wife to be a stripper. Of course, at the time he probably hadn't known that Afyon was Camille, but still . . .

Beverly went silent, and Gothabilly divided her attention between them. But at least she had the good sense not to push the issue.

Instead, she focused on Beverly's attire. "We have tons of harem dancer costumes. Let's see what we have in white." She looked through several catalogs and found a long chiffon skirt and shimmering top. "We can trim it in lace so it looks like a wedding outfit."

"That's nice," Beverly said. "But I'd prefer to switch the top to something sexier. Camille wore a breast bridle when she danced."

"Ooh. Like a chain bra with a collar? We have some of those." Gothabilly hopped up to get yet another catalog.

While she was gone, Jay cursed himself for suggesting that they dress like the historical couple. But it was too late to backpedal. Besides, he still liked the idea of being her master.

The sales clerk returned and showed them the metal bras available. Beverly chose a skimpy chain contraption decorated with sparkling beads and gold coins. Jay almost got a hard-on just looking at it.

After she picked out shoes and jewelry, they searched for masks.

Beverly favored a satin number with exotic-shaped eye-holes, sparkling stones and silky feathers, mimicking the type of disguise she'd told him that Afyon had worn. Jay chose a white domino mask with gold trim.

Once the entire order was placed, he paid the deposit, and they made an appointment to come back for a fitting.

Gothabilly thanked them, and they went on their way—with David and Camille ingrained on their minds.

CHAPTER ELEVEN

After my training was complete, the master requested that Afyon dance at a special gathering.

Baki had warned me from the beginning that harem girls often entertained in this manner, but I assumed that I would dance privately for the master my first time.

Worse yet, I was expected to disrobe. Yes, disrobe. Or more accurately, strip away my costume in front of a group of unfamiliar men while I rocked to and fro.

Soon Baki would be escorting me to the gathering, but for now, I was in the dressing room, gazing at myself in a long mirror.

My hair had been styled with a portion of it swept up and the remainder falling in loose tendrils. My mask was even more decorative than usual, glittering with precious jewels and gold-painted feathers.

My costume consisted of a billowy skirt slit high on both sides and a bridle constructed from chain that looped about my neck and caged my breasts. Laden with jewelry and a flowing sash tied around my hips, I was a sight to behold.

As Baki walked up behind me, his reflection also appeared in the mirror.

He said, "You are most exquisite."

"Thank you."

"You are an exceptional dancer, too. But fear can diminish one's abilities."

"I am not afraid." In actuality, my pulse pounded so hard, I worried that he might hear the rapid thunder. I knew how important my performance was. If I impressed the master, I would be summoned to his bedchamber later that night.

Baki did not question me further, and we proceeded to David's apartment. The gathering was being held in a lavish room designed for entertainment.

While Baki approached the master to announce my presence, I stood behind an ornately carved screen, my nervousness mounting.

The eunuch returned and told me to emerge when I heard the ringing of a small hand bell. I nodded, and he stood silently beside me.

I listened intently for my cue, my senses on full alert. The tantalizing aroma of food wafted through the room, and I realized the men would be satisfying their palates while I danced.

As the bell rang, my heart made a mad dash for my throat. Regardless, I stepped out of the shadows and into the light. Instantly, all eyes fell upon me.

I spied about ten men in total, including David. They sat on the floor in a wide circle, each of them leaning against a pillow, with a platter of delicacies beside them.

I headed toward the center, which I knew was to be my stage. As I neared my destination, I heard interested remarks about my mask. David's guests were intrigued.

That alone boosted my courage.

Upon entering the stage, I bowed to David. In this position, my bridle dangled, making my breasts more visible through the chains. His perusal of me seemed to thicken the air.

After what seemed like an appropriate amount of time, I acknowledged the other men, bowing to them, too, moving in a clockwise motion.

"She is luscious," the final one said.

I glanced up to catch my admirer's eye and noticed that he was young and handsome. The other harem girls had informed me that it was acceptable to flirt with guests, as long as I paid the master the respect he was due.

I turned in David's direction and dangled my breasts in front of him again, waiting for his order.

He popped a fig into his mouth and swallowed its sweetness. I remained poised at his disposal.

When he said, "Dance," I righted my posture, determined to win his favor.

I glanced toward the back of the room, where a trio of musicians waited. I signaled for them to play, and as the carnal rhythm began, I captured the beat, isolating the parts of my body that were on display.

I snaked my arms and jangled the chains of my bridle, but mostly the focus was on the wild vibration of my hips.

I danced around the circle, calling upon David with pagan persuasion, rolling my undulating body toward his. I teased the other men, too, giving them naughty attention.

By now, I was no longer Camille. Losing all sense of the proper princess, I became Afyon in every way.

I was alive with pleasure, blood coursing through my veins. I danced and danced, releasing Afyon's magic. She was indeed as potent as her name.

The removal of my costume came easily. I untied the sash at my waist and rubbed it against my skin. The man who had called me luscious sat forward, and I dropped it in his lap.

He brought the silky fabric to his nose, inhaling my perfumed scent. He then looped it around his neck, flaunting his treasure.

I looked at David to measure his reaction. He sat forward, too, watching me with intensity. Or was it jealousy?

Was he envious that I had not given the sash to him? Regardless, he moistened his unsmiling lips as if he hungered to kiss me.

I unhooked the top chain on my bridle, allowing the metal garment to slide down my breasts. But not entirely. I caught it before my nipples were exposed.

Exhilarated, I danced along the circle that way, taunting my captive audience. It was a lethal game, and I played it well.

Finally, I removed my breast bridle and danced topless for a short while, swaying back and forth. The tempo of the music shifted to a gentler beat.

I felt like a siren, emerging from the depths of the sea. The jewels around my nipples glimmered while overhead lanterns cast a soft glow upon my partially bared skin.

By the time I peeled away my skirt, all of the men leaned in my direction. The top of my pubis was decorated with tiny gems in the shape of a heart.

"Stunning," my admirer said.

The others voiced their approval, too. Only David remained quiet, keeping his opinion to himself.

Eager for his attention, I got down on my hands and knees and crawled over to him. While in this submissive pose, I removed the pins from my hair, unleashing the upswept portion of my henna-colored tresses.

He studied me, and I crawled closer and straddled his lap.

He grabbed my waist, quite forcefully, and held me tightly within his grasp, as if he was frustratingly bewitched.

I whispered to him in French, telling him that the heart on my pubis was for him. He seemed to understand. Not the foreign words, but the lustful invitation in my tone. Air burst from his lungs.

I worked free from his hold, stood up and turned away, my pulse pounding between my legs.

Returning to the center of the circle, I continued my naked dance. The musicians accompanied my wicked foray and the other men, especially my admirer, continued to praise me. Once again, I thrived on the power I possessed.

Upon ending my performance, I stood with my arms outstretched, immersed in my own sensuality. Then I caught David's frown. Instantly, I dropped to my knees and lowered my gaze.

Suddenly fearful of having pushed my charms too far.

On the day of the masquerade, Beverly and Jay arrived in Santa Fe and checked into a bed-and-breakfast. Although conveniently located near the historic plaza, a downtown area with restaurants, galleries, shops and museums, the B-and-B also offered a secluded garden setting.

Beverly worried that it was too romantic for a divorced couple having a short-term affair, but she didn't voice her concern.

They spent the afternoon exploring the plaza, and when dusk set in, they returned to their room to get ready for the party.

Once their transformations were complete, she stared at Jay. Between the perfectly coiled turban, the beard stubble he'd grown for the occasion, and the mask that shielded a portion of his features, he actually resembled David.

So much so, his image gave her a chill.

But she'd gone to great lengths to embody her character, too. Originally she'd intended to leave her hair as is, but at the last minute, she'd shopped for a wig the same color and style as Camille's henna-dyed locks, making Beverly look like Afyon.

"You're luscious," Jay said, giving her a start.

Luscious was the word Afyon's admirer had used to describe her. The same word David had used later that night when he'd tied a blindfolded Camille to his bed.

Was it coincidence that she and Jay were headed to a bride-and-groom-themed masque with bondage undertones? Or was it a twisted form of fate?

"What's wrong?" he asked, probably wondering why she hadn't responded to his compliment.

"Nothing," she lied. A moment later she asked, "Is this a couples-only party?"

He shook his head. "If you wouldn't have come with me, I would have gone stag. I don't know what I would have worn, though. Maybe the tux from the wedding ménage."

Beverly didn't like thinking about the night he'd played dirty honeymoon with his friends, especially since he'd done it to get his real-life marriage out of his mind.

She altered the topic. "How are Luke and Amber going to recognize you tonight?"

"I told them what we'd be wearing."

"Do you know what they'll be wearing?"

He nodded, then said, "Fancy costumes from the early 1900s. Luke is writing a screenplay that takes place in that era, so that's why they chose that time period. Knowing Amber, she'll be the belle of the ball."

No doubt, Beverly thought. Amber, she'd learned, was the jet-setting daughter of a fashion mogul. "What about Ethan? Any idea how our host will be attired?"

"He's going to be a stylized version of Frankenstein, and his girlfriend will be playing his bride."

"That's clever. What's her name?"

"Kiki. She's one of Amber's best friends. In fact, Amber set them up."

Somehow she didn't picture Amber as the matchmaker type. In fact, she preferred not to picture Amber at all.

Jay interrupted her thoughts. "We should go out front. The car will be here soon."

She nodded, aware that he'd arranged for a limo.

The chauffeur arrived, and they left the city limits and took the winding roads that led to Curtis House. At one time it had been a hilltop hotel with a decadent reputation, and now the sprawling estate was the residence of an infamous fetish artist who treated his guests to erotic fantasies.

It all seemed so surreal.

Beverly glanced out the window and saw that they were approaching an iron gate that secured the historic three-story structure.

The driver stopped at a security booth and presented their invitations, granting them entrance.

A foliage-lined driveway led to an array of towering sculptures. Nude expressions, Beverly assumed, of the man who lived there.

"Fetish art must be a lucrative business," she said.

"Ethan isn't rich from his art. He inherited his money. But he still has an impressive following from his artwork. He's a cult hero to this crowd."

The limo stopped and the chauffer opened the door and let them out. Already Beverly could hear music grinding from the house.

Before they approached the front entrance, Jay said, "I think he did some paintings that explored food fetishes. There was bondage involved, too." He made a perplexed face. "I wonder why we never experimented with anything kinky before now." Before she could respond, he answered the question himself. "I guess we were too busy being married."

She couldn't make out his expression from behind the

mask, but she suspected that he was frowning. She knew she was.

"I'm not saying that our sex life wasn't amazing," he amended. "It's just that there was so much fighting in between the fucking, we never got to the kinky stuff."

"Like silk ties and satin blindfolds?"

"Exactly."

Should she tell him about Camille's experience in that realm? Or should she reprimand him about blindfolding his ménage lover? Like the ex-wife she was, she chose the latter. "You didn't have any trouble blindfolding Amber."

"First of all, Luke was there. And secondly, she wasn't keen on the idea. Amber doesn't like giving up control."

"And you think I do?"

"You came to a party dressed as my slave, didn't you?"

"Only because Camille masqueraded as David's slave."

"Yeah, and you used to be Camille."

Touché, she thought.

He took her hand, ending their tiff. "Come on. Let's raid this shindig. I could use a drink."

"Me, too." A good, stiff one, she thought, then winced at her own double entendre.

They went inside and made their way to a massive living room, where scores of brides and grooms, in every type of costume imaginable, danced, drank and ate with abandonment.

Champagne fountains, portable bars and a lavish buffet

table heightened the festive atmosphere, but it was the stretch-ing rack—the medieval torture device—smack-dab in the middle of the room that caught Beverly's eye. She could only imagine what the dungeons housed.

"What's your pleasure?" Jay asked.

Distracted, she kept looking at the rack. Two men and one woman, all of them remarkably beautiful and lustfully at-tired, sat on the edge of it. The men, she noticed, were leaning toward each other.

"Your pleasure?" Jay asked again.

Now they were kissing, a bit roughly, a bit tenderly. "I'll take a Seven and Seven."

"You got it."

He proceeded to the nearest bar, and she stood off to the side and watched the stretching rack activity. The boy-boy thing morphed into a boy-boy-girl thing when the woman got in on the kiss.

"Do you like what you see?" a male voice asked from be-hind her.

She spun around and came face-to-face with Frankenstein. Or face to chest, considering his height. He was already tall, and combat-style platform boots added a good three inches.

She looked up at him: madly styled jet-black hair, stun-ning baby blues beneath a green eye mask, and granite-cut features. He made quite the handsome monster. The bolts on the sides of his neck were attached to a leather collar.

Beverly wasn't a BDSM expert, but in her line of work, she'd been exposed to discussions about it. And from what she understood, collars were most commonly a symbol of submission. But he seemed more like a Dominant, or a Dom, as it were.

"You must be Ethan," she said.

"And you must be Jay's wife. Sorry I don't know your name."

"It's Beverly, and I'm his ex-wife."

He politely disagreed. "You arrived together, costumed to match. Tonight you're his wife."

Oh, right, the bride-and-groom theme. Before she thought too deeply about being Jay's party wife, she changed the subject. "You have an interesting house."

He smiled. "Mission-style furniture, torture devices and erotic art?"

She nodded. "I've never seen anything like it."

"You and Jay should check out the Blue Room." He gestured toward a hallway. "It's the dungeon at the end."

"I'll keep that in mind." What else could she say? He'd already caught her watching the trio on the stretching rack.

Just then, Jay returned and handed Beverly her drink. While the men greeted each other, she spotted a woman who she assumed was Kiki—Frankenstein's bride—headed toward them.

She sported a beautifully tattered gown, and her stunning

red hair, streaked with silver, was stacked wildly on top of her head. Her half mask was the color of blood, as was her lipstick, and the collar around her neck was jeweled.

As a formal introduction was made, Beverly assumed that both Ethan and Kiki were wearing collars because they switched—a practice where the players took on either or both roles, becoming a Dom or a sub.

But when they gazed at each other, she realized it was more than that. Quite obviously, their collars were a symbol of commitment, of belonging to each other.

A pang from the past shot through Beverly's heart. They seemed crazy in love, the way she and Jay used to be.

Or could be again, she feared, if they let themselves feel too much. She chanced a look at him and discovered that he'd become engrossed in her, too.

Before a bout of awkwardness enveloped them all, Ethan and Kiki excused themselves to mingle with other guests, leaving Beverly and Jay in the midst of uncomfortable togetherness.

In the silence, they sipped their drinks and stared at each other through their masks.

Breaking the disturbing eye contact, Beverly glanced at the stretching rack. The trio was still there, only now another bride had joined them.

Drawing strength from the decadence, she said, "Ethan suggested that we visit the Blue Room."

"That's one of the dungeons."

"I know. He told me."

"Does that mean you want to watch whatever is going on?"

"Yes." Because, at the moment, she needed to focus on something that would clear her mind. Something kinky. Something crazy. Something that involved lots and lots of sex.

CHAPTER TWELVE

Before Beverly and Jay reached the Blue Room, a dashing man in a vintage suit interrupted them. On his arm was a gorgeous woman in a luxurious gown smothered in lace and embellished with red-ribbon rosettes. Her wide-brimmed hat sported a delicate veil that flirted with her pearl-trimmed mask.

Luke and Amber, Beverly thought. Even in disguise, she recognized them from the night they'd watched her dance at the club.

Luke was eerily memorable, his resemblance to Jay undeniable. They had the same mouth, the same chin, the same hard-cut jaw.

And Amber had slept with both of them.

Beverly turned and locked gazes with her. A beat of silence passed before an introduction was made.

Afterward, the men walked a few feet away and started shooting the breeze, deliberately leaving the women to fend for themselves.

Cowards, Beverly thought.

Amber spoke first. "You're a redhead tonight." She scanned the length of Beverly's costume. "A harem bride. A dancer. You're as breathtaking as you were on stage."

"Thank you." Beverly had been prepared to dislike Jay's former lover, but it was difficult to dislike someone who paid you a compliment. "Jay said that you would be the belle of the ball, and you are."

The brunette smiled. "It's my ball."

That was true. This was her wild-spirited engagement party. "Your gown is beautiful. I can't imagine what you're going to wear at your real wedding."

"Me, neither." Amber laughed. She had a spoiled, rich girl air about her. Even her European-tinged accent dripped with money. "But I'll come up with something that will blow everyone away." She leaned in close. "You're not bothered by what we did, are you? Luke and I are aware that Jay told you about it."

Clearly, she was referring to the threesome, making Beverly fumble for a response.

"I guess that means you are bothered," Amber said.

"A little." At this point, it seemed foolish to lie. "But I know I shouldn't be. It's not as if I was part of Jay's life at the time."

"I didn't even know he had an ex-wife when I first met him. I didn't know much about Luke, either. They were both a bit of a mystery. Did Jay tell you about the night we all played Truth or Dare?"

"No." Beverly glanced over at the men. They were still out of earshot. "Did something significant happen?"

Amber nodded. "Luke dared me to pretend I was someone other than myself. So I stood naked in front of them and described my imaginary appearance." She made a full-body gesture. "And guess what? I came up with a description that was a dead ringer for you, right down to the stripper part. Only at the time, I didn't know what you looked like or that you were a dancer."

"Wow." It certainly wasn't what Beverly had expected to hear.

"Jay didn't tell me that I'd unwittingly described you. Instead he made dirty love to me and fantasized that I was you."

Beverly drew a quick breath. She didn't know how to feel about Jay being inside someone else while he was thinking about her.

Amber spoke again. "You can see why I was so curious about you and why Luke and I came to see you dance."

"That was a strange experience for me. I had no idea who either of you were, but Luke's resemblance to Jay gave me a start."

"I know. We could tell. It was obvious that you weren't over Jay. That's part of why we encouraged him to reconnect with you."

"We're not in love anymore," Beverly clarified. "It's just an affair. In fact, we were on our way to one of the dungeons when we ran into you."

Amber lifted her ladylike veil and peered directly through her mask. "To watch something kinky?"

"The kinkier the better."

The brunette didn't mince words. "So you're using sex in place of love?"

Dang, Beverly thought. Did the other woman have to be so astute? "I didn't say I was doing that."

"You didn't have to. Believe me, I've been there. I did whatever I could to fight my feelings for Luke."

"It isn't the same. You're getting married, and we're divorced. If we try to get back together, all of those old arguments will flare up again. Jay can't handle my job, and I can't deal with his possessiveness."

"Then go to the dungeon and have a good time. But if you think he was possessive before, just imagine how he's going to react when he gets a whiff of Doms in action with their subs. He's going to want to own you for sure."

"I'm willing to let him possess me in bed." It was keeping her heart safe that mattered.

~

After my performance, I donned my clothes and Baki escorted me back to the harem, where we waited for word from the master. Sarila and Ruby waited with us, chattering about inconsequential things. I knew they were trying to keep me busy, but I was unable to focus on anything save David.

Hours later, the harem bell sounded and Baki leaped up to meet with the master and acquire my fate.

While the eunuch was gone, my instructors continued to chatter, and I folded my quaking hands on my lap.

"The master is going to want you tonight," Sarila said. "How can he not?" She smiled, trying to reassure me. "Look how stunning you are."

"Yes, but the way I performed. They way I straddled him without his permission. He probably thinks I have the devil inside me."

"A she-devil he will not be able to resist," Ruby remarked.

How I hoped they were right. "What is taking Baki so long?"

Sarila reached over to pat my folded hands. "It has only been a matter of minutes."

When the eunuch finally arrived, my instructors dashed to

their feet. I remained seated, too nervous to move. Glancing up, I searched Baki's gaze.

He said, "You won the master's favor."

My breath rushed out, freeing my constricted lungs.

Ruby and Sarila clapped like silly schoolgirls, and Baki silenced them with a look.

"There is more," he proclaimed.

I gestured for him to continue and he said, "You are to remain as you are, attired in your dancewear. And I have been instructed to cover your eyes with a strip of cloth before I escort you to the master's bedchamber."

My pulse jumped. "A blindfold? Did the master say for what purpose?"

"No, he did not."

Ruby had a suggestion. "Maybe he is going to surprise you with a gift."

"Yes," Sarila said. "He often rewards us with gifts when we do something that impresses him. I received a necklace for my service on your wedding night."

I tilted my head. "He gave you jewels for taking my place?"

She winced, realizing her blunder. This was not the time to discuss my debauched wedding night.

I turned to Baki. "Is it possible that he intends to punish me for my performance? And the blindfold is to keep me from seeing the blows he will inflict?"

"The master has never whipped a slave before."

"I could be the first."

Sarila interjected, "The master is a just man."

Ruby agreed. "He would never harm you."

I prayed that they knew best. "Then go. Find a suitable blindfold. Something that complements my costume."

They dashed off to the wardrobe room.

While they were gone Baki said, "The master might be planning to punish you in a carnal way."

Not quite understanding, I blinked at him. Then it dawned on me, and my skin went hot. "Are you saying that he will do wicked things to me while my eyes are swathed?"

"It is possible."

Suddenly I was even more nervous. But I feigned a smile. "At least I am being called to his bedchamber."

Ruby and Sarila rejoined us with a lovely sash to use as my blindfold. Baki wrapped the thick satin fabric over my mask, pressing it tightly to the feathers.

Upon tying a knot at the back of my head, he asked, "Is your vision blocked?"

"Yes, completely."

The girls bade me good-bye, and Baki took my arm, guiding me outside.

I held on to him, clutching his muscles. I could only imagine how being this close to David was going to feel. A sexual encounter, even a perverse one, was certainly more appealing than being whipped.

Or so I hoped.

I breathed in the night air, and as we walked through the courtyard, I nearly stumbled on a stone beneath my slipper. Baki steadied me before I fell.

Upon entering the building that led to David's apartment, I muttered in French, reminding myself that I was Afyon and not Camille. At the moment, I felt more like a scorned wife than a seductive harem girl.

"Do you think he is suspicious?" I asked.

"Suspicious of what?"

"Who I actually am."

"If he was, why would he have arranged for you to remove your clothing for other men? I see no reason for that."

"Nor do I." But my mind was scattered. Nothing seemed to make sense. "Has he ever inflicted carnal punishment before?"

"Not that I am aware of."

"Then why would he do it to me?"

"I only said that it was a possibility."

A likely one, I thought. Or else the eunuch would not have mentioned it.

He stopped, bringing me to an abrupt halt.

"What is the matter?" I asked.

"Nothing. We are here."

I held fast to his arm. "What happens now?"

"I was instructed to knock, then walk away."

I panicked. "You are going to leave me? Alone in the hallway? What if he never comes out to fetch me?"

"He will. But if it gives you comfort, I can walk slowly."

I wanted to beg Baki to stay. This was worse than my wedding night.

He applied the knocker, rapping loudly. Then he let go of me and said, "Be well."

His footsteps sounded, slowly, as promised. But that did little to ease my fears. He was moving farther and farther away.

I was tempted to remove the blindfold and chase after him, but I stayed strong and waited for David to grant me entrance. I even lifted my chin, trying to appear confident, like a courageous woman on her way to the gallows.

Then it happened. His heavy wooden door creaked open.

"Afyon," David said, his voice deep and familiar.

"Master," I responded. Tonight, of all nights, I was truly his slave.

He took my hand and led me inside. When I heard the door snap shut behind us, my heartbeat accelerated to a spinning pace.

"Do you know why I brought you here?" he asked.

"To surprise me with a gift," I said.

He laughed beneath his breath. "Is that what you truly think is going to occur?"

I shook my head.

He released my hand. "Are you frightened?"

"Yes." False bravado was getting me nowhere.

"Then you must be aware that I intend to punish you."

"It crossed my mind," I responded, keeping my conversation with Baki private.

"And what would you say is your offense?"

"My performance was too bold."

"Yes, it was. But it was thrilling, too. You made my cock hard."

Warmth spread between my legs. "Then why am I being subject to penalty?"

"Because I spent the remainder of the evening refusing Sheikh Hayri's offers to purchase you."

"The man who openly admired me?"

"He is my boyhood friend, and his obsession to have you nearly caused a rift between us." David moved closer, his sandalwood scent accosting my senses. "A woman should never create that kind of friction."

"I had not meant to."

"You should still be punished." Without warning, he pulled me roughly against him, his mouth crushing down upon mine.

Our first kiss.

It felt so wrong yet so horribly right, I wanted to weep. His tongue pushed past my lips, his skin radiating from beneath his clothes.

We kissed and kissed, and as my heart thudded against his, he unhooked my breast bridle and removed it from my body. He tugged my skirt down my hips, too. What lovely punishment, I thought. Being naked for my master's amusement.

Then I heard him ripping something apart. My skirt?

Confused, I flinched. Why was he destroying my clothes?

"Get into bed," he said, turning me in the direction in which I was to go.

As I began to walk, taking slow and cautious steps, he told me to "crawl."

I got down on my hands and knees. Was he watching the sway of my bare bottom as I moved? I was both embarrassed and aroused by the position I was in.

As I proceeded across the runner that led to his bed, his footsteps sounded behind me. Shrouded in darkness, I bumped into the bed. Reaching for the platform, I lifted myself up.

He said, "Lie down and put your arms above your head."

Once again, I obeyed. The bedding was soft and silky against my exposed flesh, but I was far from comfortable, especially when he grabbed one of my wrists and tied it to the nearest post. I suspected that he was using a strip from my shredded skirt to bind me. After securing my other wrist, he tied my ankles together.

As he climbed onto the bed and planted his knees on either side of my face, I held my breath. The weight of his body dipped into the mattress.

I envisioned him looking down at me, his power-laden gaze fixed on my blindfold.

"Sheikh Hayri described you well. You are luscious indeed." He shifted his knee-stance as if preparing to get closer. "Do you enjoy being my slave?"

"Yes" was all I could manage to say.

"Have you been practicing how to pleasure me?"

"Yes," I said again. "With an olisbos."

"How deeply can you take it?"

"Almost all the way." No matter how I tried, I had yet to conquer the full length. Regardless, Ruby and Sarila insisted that I should be proud.

"Almost? Hmm." He did not sound impressed. "You will have to do better than that."

"I can try."

"Try," he mocked. "You will do exactly as I say."

How? I thought. I had been sucking on the damnable olisbos day and night. "What if I fail?"

"Do you crave my punishment, Afyon? Is that why you never cease to challenge me?"

"I am sorry, Master." I had not meant to defy him, especially while I was trussed to his bed. But I was his lovesick wife, struggling to be his slave.

He rebuffed my apology. "Maybe I should sell you to Hayri. Praise be to Allah, it would be good to be rid of you."

"No, please. I will do whatever you want. Just keep me as your own."

"Then pleasure me." He removed my blindfold so that I could look up at him. "All the way," he added, as he loosened his pants, giving me a close-up view of his penis.

Hard and thick and ready for my mouth.

CHAPTER THIRTEEN

The Blue Room had been aptly named. The walls were a wild shade of cobalt and the mosaic floors sizzled with an array of blue tiles.

A portion of the room provided luxury: velvet sofas, satin pillows, lush window trimmings and pretty antiques.

The rest of the décor created the dungeon: metal cages, wooden racks, suspension slings, padded tables with metal rings, stockades and every other type of BDSM furniture one could imagine.

Beverly took a moment to catch her breath. Other guests cluttered the sofas, watching a variety of sexual activity. It was like being on the set of a porno, but without the cameras, the director or the crew.

Jay reached for her hand, and she threaded her fingers through his, grateful for his familiar touch.

Immersed in the strange atmosphere, she spied a girl in the center of the dungeon, dressed as an erotic angel, bending over and lifting her skirt so that a man in a demonic mask could spank her.

"There's no place to sit," Jay said, indicating that the sofas were full.

Beverly glanced at the demon's wicked leer. "Then maybe we should leave."

"You don't want to watch?"

She shifted her gaze to a woman in a Cinderella costume and glittery mask. Prince Charming was strapping her to a table. "Maybe we can stay for a few minutes."

Jay guided her closer to the activity, where they stood behind one of the sofas.

Offbeat as some of them were, all of the players were portraying brides and grooms. Beverly took a second look at the angel. She seemed too delicate to be the demon's bride, but apparently that was the point of their scene. Her wedding veil fluttered softly, and her pert little bottom was as red as a hot poker.

In another section of the dungeon a ménage took center stage. Aside from their masks, all that was left of their clothes were bow ties on the men and lace panties and high heels on the woman.

She was quite the dominatrix, wielding a whip and snap-

ping it on the floor while she instructed her grooms to call her
"Mistress."

Beverly preferred Cinderella and Prince Charming. Bondage had never seemed so sweet. He was leaning over her, kissing her romantically on the mouth.

"You like that scene," Jay said quietly.

"Apparently so do you," she responded just as softly. He,
too, was watching the fairy-tale couple.

He defended his choice. "I just want to see him climb on
her face."

"He isn't going to do that."

"Yes, he is. I can tell that's what he's after."

She looked at the prince. Tall and trim, with a regal smile, he
sported a sleek satin mask. "He seems gentlemanly to me."

"Yeah, you just wait."

Wait she did, watching everything. After kissing his captive, he walked around the table to tighten her restraints.
Okay, so maybe he did have something rough in mind.

"You're probably right," Beverly said.

"Of course I am. This isn't child's play."

No, but the fairy-tale spin made it seem okay somehow.

Charming loosened the front of Cinderella's ball gown,
pushing her bountiful breasts to the surface. Beverly couldn't
help being intrigued.

Jay smiled. "Ah, there he goes."

Sure enough, Charming climbed onto the table.

Beverly's heart dipped and dived. "Lord, this is sexy."

"It is, isn't it?" Jay moved to stand behind her.

"What are you doing?"

"Holding you." He slipped his arms around her.

Caught up in the moment, she leaned back against him. He was impossible to resist, and so, heaven forbid, was the other couple.

"I'll bet they're really married," Jay said,

"What makes you think so?" Charming straddled Cinderella's face, but he didn't unbutton his breeches, at least not yet.

"They're both wearing wedding rings."

"Those could be props. Or they could be swingers, married to other people."

"Not with the way they're looking at each other."

"Like they're in love?" She took a choppy breath. "We looked at each other that way earlier."

"Yes, and we used to feel that way."

Used to? Or still did? While Beverly struggled with her thoughts, Cinderella stared adoringly at her man.

"This is wrong," Beverly said.

"What is? Watching other people get off? They like it. They want us to be their audience."

She was talking about her and Jay being tender exes. If he hadn't been so wrapped up in the scene, he would have understood.

Charming finally undid his breeches, but it was Jay who

snared Beverly's attention. He lifted the front of her harem skirt and worked his hand into her panties.

Oh, God. "You can't do that," she whispered.

"I already am," he whispered back. "Besides, no one can see. The couch is blocking us."

"I know, but . . ."

He rubbed her clit in soft little circles. "Just enjoy the show, and I'll take care of the rest."

Beverly sighed, and Charming pushed down his pants and positioned himself over Cinderella's mouth.

"David did that to Camille," she said.

"Did what, baby?"

"Tied her up and made her give him a blowjob."

"Damn. Really?" Jay applied more pressure.

A sinful sound escaped Beverly's lips. Her clit throbbed. "He made her take all of him, every inch."

"I hope our guy up there gives it to her that way."

"Me, too." Charming was nicely endowed.

As if on cue, the prince pushed Cinderella's mouth open, his balls pressing against her.

"Dirty boy," Jay said.

"Who? You or him?"

"Him. But I'm feeling dirty, too. Turn your face so I can kiss you."

She wasn't about to refuse. While they kissed, he slipped a finger inside and made her deliciously wet.

Sounds of S and M rang in her ears: the angel being spanked, the dominatrix bride snapping her long, white whip.

Jay ended the kiss and told her to watch the fairy-tale scene, which she did. As Charming found his rhythm, Beverly squirmed against Jay's hand. He put a second finger inside her.

"Look at her shoe," he said.

Beverly glanced at Cinderella's feet. One of her glass slippers dangled from her toes.

As if working his way toward the stroke of midnight, Charming thrust deeper. Cinderella kicked off her shoe and moaned her pleasure. Clearly, she liked being overpowered by her man.

And so did Beverly. Between watching the storybook couple and falling prey to Jay's charms, she couldn't get enough. She was already starting to spasm.

Jay nipped her ear. "It's happening to him, too."

As Beverly slammed into clitoral ecstasy, Prince Charming unleashed the full extent of his hunger, spilling hard and fast into his ladylove's mouth.

~

I was bound to David's bed like a prisoner, yet somewhere deep inside, I was dangerously aroused.

While he remained poised above me, I looked up at his face and marveled at his masculine beauty. His catlike eyes shimmered in the soft light.

Preparing to be pleasured, he removed his shirt and cast it aside. He shoved his pants down farther, too. Then, as if to tease me, he put his erection marvelously close to my lips.

I darted out my tongue, and that simple action made his penis twitch. Tentatively, I connected with the tip, and his stomach muscles jumped in anticipation. I grew bolder and swirled my tongue, flirting with the tip.

I licked him again, and a drop of his seed oozed out. He tasted wilder than the mixture I had been drinking. Another drop appeared, and I suspected that when he experienced his full release, the fluid would be plentiful.

He watched me, and I watched him. He looked quite princely, kneeling over my face with his testes drawn tight. If my hands had been free, I would have cupped them.

I opened my mouth, and he pushed his penis inside. But he did not go far. He was building a foundation for his excitement.

I accommodated him, suckling the portion given to me. Nursing him was different than nursing an olisbos. He was warmer than the wood, hard yet pliable, silkier than I had imagined. He pushed a bit deeper and created a stroking sensation.

In and out he went, and I relaxed my throat, making his mission smoother.

He lewdly said, "Do you like having your master's cock in your mouth?"

I knew it was a question for which no response was required. He was merely exhibiting his power.

And that aroused me even more. Warmth spread through my bound body, heating my blood. Down below, my heart-jeweled vulva went moist. I squirmed and tried to lift my bottom in the air.

Demanding my attention, he purposefully thrust deeper, forcing me to focus on him.

"Your jaw is going to ache when I finish with you," he said.

A dull throb had already begun to set in, but I cared not. While in training, I had swallowed the olisbos until I was sore, preparing for a moment such as this.

No, not quite like this, I amended.

He leaned forward, setting a stronger rhythm, and our gazes met and held.

He puzzled over me. "How can you look so unabashed yet so innocent?"

Because that was how I felt, I thought. Wickedly beholden to the man I loved.

Without warning, he cupped my head, pulled me closer and pushed all the way in, hitting the back of my throat.

He thrust back and forth, claiming his victory. I felt victorious, too. To intensify his experience, I swirled my tongue, teasing the underside of his shaft.

He nearly spilled into me. But he caught himself before it happened and slowed his pace.

In the interim, he touched my face, gently, almost lovingly.

My heart hit my chest. Was he growing fond of me? Had I become part of him?

He seemed to be thinking the same thing, and apparently he was not pleased with his thoughts. A troubled expression furrowed his brow.

Still frowning, he increased the tempo once again, keeping his promise to make my jaw ache. With rough emotion, he used me for as long as he could endure.

When his loins tensed and his body jerked, I prepared for the rush of ejaculate, knowing this was the onset of his climax.

He made a dark, primal sound, and as he spilled his seed, I swallowed what he issued.

After he recovered, he reclined next to me, intimate silence stretching between us.

Finally I asked, "Are you going to untie me now?"

He looked my way. "No."

"You intend to punish me some more?"

"No, Afyon. I am replete for the night."

"Then when are you going to release me?"

"Sometime tomorrow."

"Tomorrow?" Frustrated by his casual air, I struggled against my bonds. Maybe I was wrong about his feelings for me, maybe he did not care at all. "You cannot possibly leave me this way until then."

"I can and I will." *He rolled over, intent on getting his sleep and reminding me, quite effectively, that he was the master and I was the slave.*

⌒

After the party, Jay and Beverly rode back to the B-and-B in the limo. He was horny as hell, but confused, too. He felt oddly emotional, only he wasn't sure why.

Beverly got his attention. "Don't you want to know what's in there?"

He glanced at the unopened grab bag on his lap. Everyone at the party had received one as a parting gift. Beverly had already torn into hers. She'd gotten a box of X-rated candy: fruit-flavored peckers and gummy boobs.

"I'd rather wait to open mine when we're in the room," he said.

"Why should that matter?"

"In case I get something that makes me hard."

She didn't accept his reasoning. "You've been hard most of the night."

Was it any wonder? Between watching Cinderella swallow the prince's sword and fingering Beverly until she came, he was due for a climax of his own.

"Okay. Here goes." He tore the ribbon off the bag and opened it. Digging around to examine the contents, he smiled, suddenly grateful for the diversion.

Beverly leaned forward in her seat, which was a safe distance from his. "Don't keep me in suspense."

"It's a bunch of different kinds of rope."

"Rope?" She made a face. "So much for silk ties and satin blindfolds."

"Don't despair." He removed a book from the bag. "There's an instruction manual." He patted the seat next to him. "Come over here and check it out."

She seemed leery, but he supposed that he couldn't blame her. They were just learning to get kinky with each other. Then again, it wasn't as if she was a complete innocent.

He said, "For a girl who works in the sex industry, you're not very daring."

She jumped to her own defense. "You expect me to trust you with a bag of rope? You can barely tie a necktie."

He grinned. She had him there. "Who gives a shit about a Windsor knot or half Windsor or whatever?" He waved the book. "This is what every guy needs to know."

She managed a good-humored laugh. "Okay. I'm game. For looking at the manual," she clarified. "I'll need a bit more convincing for the actual rope part."

He rolled his eyes. "Just get over here."

She moved to sit beside him, and he adjusted the book so they could both see it.

"There's an entire chapter on safety," he said, trying to reassure her.

She turned to another section. "Yikes. Who knew there were so many different spread-eagle positions?"

"I think this is hot." He showed her illustrations of female breast and genital bondage.

"Hmm," she said.

Did that mean she liked it? Or didn't? "Are you deliberately trying to drive me crazy?"

"Maybe." She smiled and kissed him squarely on the mouth.

Crazy, he decided, had never tasted so good. He tugged her closer. He was going to dominate the hell out of her tonight.

Later, he learned, that was easier said than done. Once they got back to their room and changed out of their costumes and put on their robes, he sat at the dining table stressing over his task.

Beverly sat next to him. "Having trouble?"

"No," he lied.

"You are, too."

He glanced up from the square knot he'd bungled. "Okay, so maybe a little."

"Here." She took the rope and fixed his knot. She explained, "I used to macramé when I was a kid. I even won some ribbons for my work."

Christ, he thought. Did she have to be such an expert? "How seventies of you."

"Don't get testy. I can teach you."

"To make wall hangings?"

Beverly laughed. "To tie me up."

He laughed, too. There was no point in losing his sense of humor. "That's just what a Dom wants. His sub giving him lessons."

"In BDSM they say that power flows from the bottom up. A Dom can't do anything without the sub's permission."

She was right. He'd read that in the book. "Okay, then let's do this."

With some practice pieces, she taught him how to tie a variety of basic knots, which was all he needed to know.

Once he felt confident to move on, he followed the instructions in the manual, measuring and cutting a piece of rope for her breasts. He used nail polish—a trick of the bondage trade—on the ends to keep them from fraying, and prepared another piece for her genitals.

"The book says that we're supposed to choose a safe word," he said. "A code to end the activity if it becomes too much for you. And don't pick *no* because in this type of play, no doesn't always mean no."

"You're really taking this to the letter."

"Better safe than sorry. Now choose a word."

"How about macramé?"

"Seriously?"

"It's as good as any."

He supposed it was. Eager to play, Jay gave his first order. "Stand up and drop your robe."

"Yes, Master," she said, teasing him with feigned subservience.

"Don't get smart. Just do it."

She sobered, probably from his no-nonsense tone. Lowering her garment, she displayed full-frontal nudity at its finest. He got aroused just looking at her. But he didn't disrobe. That would come later.

He went to work on her breasts, binding them together while he tied her arms behind her back.

"What does it feel like?" he asked.

"It's the strangest bra I've ever worn."

"Get used to it." With her big, stripper boobs, it worked extremely well. He lowered his head to lick her nipples, switching back and forth and making them stand at attention.

As a sweet little sigh escaped her lips, Jay blew on the wet spots he'd made. He was totally digging this.

Anxious to bind her genitals, he wrapped a rope around her waist, along her hip bones and through her labia. He finished with a knot pressed against her clit.

She caught her breath. "You're getting good at this."

"I'm a quick study."

"I'll say." She squirmed against the knot. "What happens now?"

"I'm going to make you get on your knees." Prince Charming had gotten his way with his woman and, according to Beverly, so had Prince David. Now Jay wanted his turn.

He waited to see if she was willing. Thankfully, she was. She didn't use the safe word.

He removed his robe, sat on the edge of the bed, and opened his legs. He was already raging hard.

She moved closer, and he motioned for her to kneel between his thighs. She complied, wrapping her mouth around him.

He cupped the back of her head and pushed deeper, taking as much pleasure as he could.

She looked up at him. His ex-wife, he thought. The woman he'd once loved. Beautifully bound.

And giving him exactly what he craved.

CHAPTER FOURTEEN

I awakened in the pitch of darkness and felt David leaning over me. I squinted at his shadow. Was he going to incite another sexual encounter, even though he had claimed earlier that he was replete for the night?

He reached up, and I realized that he was releasing my bonds. I stirred to let him know that I was aware of him.

He said, "You have been fitful."

This was true. Exhausted as I was, being restrained hindered my sleep.

He proceeded to untie my ankles, and once I was completely free, I moved my arms and legs to combat the stiffness.

"Now we can rest," he said.

Allowing myself the luxury of his proximity, I scooted closer to him. Content, I closed my eyes, his breath warm against my skin.

In the morning, he was leaning over me again. Only this time I could see him fully in the light. He was slightly mussed from sleep, his dark hair spilling across his forehead.

"You molted," he said.

Puzzled, I blinked at him.

"You lost your feathers, like a bird. Most of your jewels fell off, too." He held up the tip of his finger, where he had captured a tiny gem. "The only part of your sparkle that remains intact is down there." He indicated the heart on my pubis.

Uncertain of how to respond, I kept quiet.

"The kohl around your eyes is smeared," he went on to say. "But not enough to unmask you."

I breathed easier. "It is not time to reveal myself to you."

"When will be the time?"

"When the cut around my eye heals," I reminded him.

"It must be a stubborn wound."

"It is. I am bandaged beneath the kohl," I lied.

"I cannot see it."

"It is cleverly disguised."

He studied me intently before he asked, "Are you aware of your likeness to my wife?"

In an attempt to maintain my composure, I cleared my throat. As always, I worried that he had become suspicious of my identity. "Your wife?"

"*The princess I married. Surely you know of her.*"

"*Of course. But no one informed me about a likeness.*" I attempted to think like a harem girl, saying something a slave might say. "*Which of us is more beautiful?*"

David continued to study me. "*Until I see you without your mask, I am unable to answer that question.*"

I feigned envy over myself. "*I hope you find me more pleasurable than you do her.*" Playing my Afyon part, I trailed the tip of the feather along his chest and down his stomach.

He caught my hand before I tickled his penis, which had begun to stir to life.

"*Open your legs,*" he said.

Naturally, I obeyed him.

"*Wider,*" he commanded.

Once again I did as I was told. While I lay there, spread out for his view, I tried to envision how I looked. I suspected that I made a wanton image with my mask smeared and my pubis shimmering with last night's jewels.

He got out of bed and returned with an olisbos, only it was made out of ivory instead of wood.

"*This was a gift from an emperor,*" he said. "*It was commissioned as an art piece. I want you to use it.*"

He handed the phallus to me, and I studied the lifelike object. It was magnificently carved.

I assumed that he wanted me to insert it into my vagina. Why else would he have ordered me to open my legs?

I hesitated. "It needs to be lubricated."

He responded, "I will provide the necessary oil. But first, you shall make yourself wet."

As he moved to the foot of the bed to watch, I slid a hand between my wide-spread legs, my pulse pounding at the crux of my thighs.

I rubbed softly, creating pinpoints of pleasure. To intensify my experience, I brought the tip of the olisbos to my lips and licked it.

My husband's breath escaped his lungs.

I smiled to myself and licked the olisbos again, the ivory cool against my tongue. Soon I was nursing the head, imagining that it was him. He seemed to be envisioning the same thing. He groaned when I made a suckling sound.

As my vagina grew moist, I parted my folds, opening myself like a flower and giving him an explicit view.

I rubbed and rubbed, feeling downright scandalous. Unable to control myself, I moaned and sighed and climaxed.

Afterward, I removed the phallus from my mouth, and he grabbed it and tossed it aside.

He no longer wanted me to copulate with the olisbos. He entered me instead, and we made frantic love, rolling over the bed.

I landed on his lap, and he clutched my waist and lifted me up and down. It was like riding a big, bucking stallion.

Soon, he repositioned me, putting me on my hands and knees and treating me like a mare in heat.

He got behind me, steadied his hands on my hips and thrust deep. I gasped, then clutched a bedpost, the same one to which I had been tied.

Maintaining a fast, hard rhythm, he buried his face in my hair. I could feel him breathing in my scent.

But as aroused as he was, he seemed frustrated, too.

At the height of his release, he reached forward and attacked the pattern on my pubis. Catching the underside of the jewels with his fingernails, he scraped my skin.

Chipping away the heart I had created for him.

Jay leaned over Beverly while she slept. He had no concept of how long he'd been watching her, but he couldn't seem to stop staring.

The ropes he'd bound her with last night were coiled on the floor, reminding him of their rough play. And now that it was over, now that daylight was shooting through the window sheers, he felt more like a slave than a master.

A slave to what? His heart? God, he hoped not.

Jay cursed his frustration. Why did everything have to be so complicated? Why couldn't he just have some fun with his ex and be done with it?

Beverly's lashes flitted, but before she opened her eyes, he moved away from her, not wanting to get caught staring.

She came awake, sat up and blinked. Outwardly, he maintained his cool.

"Hey," he said.

"Hi." The sheet slipped to her waist, and she stretched her arms above her head, comfortable in her nudity.

Jay wanted to tie her up again, to ask her submit to him one last time. But he curbed his machismo and let it go.

A few minutes later, her stomach growled and she said, "I guess I didn't eat enough at the party."

He considered making a crack about the protein she'd consumed afterward, but he figured that would be in bad taste. Literally. "This place offers a free continental breakfast. Should I order it?"

"Yes, please, that sounds great."

While he made the call, Beverly went into the bathroom and returned with her face washed, her hair combed, and her teeth brushed. Then she put on a tank top and a pair of shorts.

Jay got cleaned up, too, and when breakfast arrived, they climbed back into bed with a basket of baked goods.

He went after a bagel, which he smothered in cream cheese, and she decided on an oatmeal raisin muffin, which she ate between sips of orange juice.

As cozy as the moment was, it didn't help. His mind wandered back to his troubled feelings. "Have you told your past-life therapist about your affair with me?"

"Yes, I have, and she was intrigued, especially when I told her that I thought you might be David."

He struggled not to frown. "When we were together before, I used to think of you as my soul mate. But it was just a phrase I used. Besides, how could you be my soul mate if we split up? That doesn't make much sense."

"Actually, it does." She dropped crumbs onto her lap. "Some soul mates live harmoniously. But sometimes, depending on the issues involved, they don't end up resolving their differences. And when that happens, they have to let go and move on until they're reunited in another life."

"You mean we might have to do this again?"

"Can you imagine? But you know what else? We don't have just one soul mate. We have lots of them, and the relationships aren't always based on romantic love. Friends, family, even pets can be soul mate connections."

"Pets?"

"That's what my therapist said. I learned all of this from her."

He pondered the information. "Maybe I'll come back in my next life as your dog."

"And maybe you're already a dog in this life."

He pinched her. "Smart aleck."

She laughed, then said, "Have you ever heard of a twin flame?"

He shook his head. "No. What is it?"

"A twin flame is the other half of your soul."

His curiosity piqued. "Meaning what, exactly?"

"Supposedly twin flames were one entity that separated into two beings—one masculine and one feminine. Sometimes they spend their lives together, but mostly they're apart. It's the strongest form of a spiritual connection, and they have to be ready for it. The purpose of twins coming together is for some kind of spiritual service work. If they haven't evolved to that level, it won't work."

"That rules us out. We're about as underdeveloped as it gets."

"Speak for yourself."

"Oh, right, Miss Stripper. You won't even go to church for fear of being judged."

"Okay. So you have a point." She dug into the basket for another muffin. "But this conversation is useless unless you get regressed."

He shook his head. "Don't start in about that."

She pressed the issue. "I want to know for sure if you're David."

"And I'd rather not make this thing between us any worse than it already is."

"What's that supposed to mean?"

"It means that I don't want to be your tortured soul mate or your undeveloped twin flame or whatever else David might have been to Camille."

She turned testy. "When I first got regressed, it didn't even occur to me that David could be you."

He got snippy, too. "So?"

"So you're the one who popped back into my life. You're the one who showed up at the club wanting a private dance."

He didn't like that she'd laid the blame on him. "Yeah, and we both agreed on a sex-only affair."

She glared at him. "I'm not changing the rules."

"Then why are we arguing?" He lowered the tone of his voice, trying to ease the situation back to normal, even if their relationship was far from normal.

His cell phone rang, and he jumped to answer it. On the other line was Amber.

After the customary hello, she said, "Will you ask Beverly if she wants to have lunch with Kiki and me today? We'll only steal her away from you for a few hours."

"You can ask her yourself." He gave Bev the phone, hoping she accepted the invitation. He figured a slight separation would do them some good.

Apparently she agreed. When the afternoon rolled around, she got ready for her outing. And although their tiff had ended, he was still steeped in the turmoil of reconnecting with his ex.

In any life.

～

Amber sent a Town Car for Beverly, and she was chauffeured to an impressive Spanish Colonial Revival mansion owned by Amber's fashion designer mother.

Upon arrival, she was escorted to a café table in the midst of a flourishing rose garden.

Amber and Kiki greeted her. Kiki looked soft and pretty in the light of day with long, wavy red hair spilling over her shoulders and freckles dusting her nose. Amber, as always, looked model chic with a brunette bob and stylish clothes.

Amber indicated the southwestern fare on the table: festive salads with honey chipotle dressing and chili-chicken enchiladas served with rice, black beans and pico de gallo. For dessert: lemon flan garnished with fresh berries.

They sat down, and Amber poured each of them a glass of iced tea. "I hope you're hungry," she said to Beverly.

"I am." She hadn't eaten since cramming a few muffins into her mouth with Jay. She looked around. "This is a beautiful setting."

Amber smiled. "Luke inspired my love of roses."

"Jay told me about how often Luke gives you red roses."

"We'll probably be married here. A garden ceremony seems fitting." The bride-to-be draped a napkin across her lap. "Did Jay also tell you that he was known as Pink?"

"Yes, from the pink boutonniere he wore on the night you . . ."

"Had our first ménage?" Amber spoke candidly. "We've come a long way since then. He's going to give me away at my wedding."

"He is?" Now that Beverly hadn't known. "I would have pegged him for the best man, but not the father of the bride, so to speak."

"He's the man I trust most in this world, besides Luke, of course. My fathers, all four of them, aren't worth my time, let alone deserving of an honorable place in my wedding."

Beverly understood. She had family issues of her own.

Kiki chimed into the conversation. She asked Beverly, "Where were you and Jay married?"

"At the beach. But that seems like a lifetime ago."

"You looked enamored of each other last night."

"It's complicated." Beverly didn't know how else to describe it.

"I understand complicated," Kiki said. She was minus the jeweled collar today. "When Ethan and I first got together, his house was haunted. Not only were we struggling with our relationship, we were trying to help two lovelorn ghosts find their way back to each other."

"Oh, wow. And here I thought our situation was odd."

"You mean the past-life stuff?" This from Amber. "Jay mentioned it, but he didn't go into detail. Why don't you fill me and Kiki in? We'd love to know what it's all about."

Beverly started at the beginning and told them everything

about Camille and David. The other women ate while she talked. Beverly enjoyed the food, too, and by the time she finished her tale, the three of them were on dessert.

"So that's why you were dressed as a harem bride and a Middle Eastern prince," Kiki said.

Beverly spooned into the pudding. "The costumes were Jay's idea. He wanted me to be his slave."

The redhead grinned. "I can't blame him there."

Amber interjected, "He has to be David's incarnate. There are too many coincidences for him not to be." She gave a slight pause. "It's interesting that Camille wore a henna pattern on her hands."

"It's a bridal tradition. So is having the groom's name hidden in the pattern."

"I know. My mother's friend, Yasmine, is a mehndi artist here in Santa Fe. She does henna tattoos for parties, but she does traditional designs, too. I could give her a call and see if she's available right now. We could all get something."

"I'm game." Kiki polished off her flan. "Maybe I could have my nipples done."

Amber laughed. "Ethan would love that." To Beverly she said, "How about you? Do you want to get painted? Your hands, not your boobs."

Beverly put her spoon down and felt the hands in question tremble. "It's already giving me a sense of déjà vu."

Amber spoke again. "You could have Jay's name hidden in the design."

Heaven help her, she wanted to, but the very idea scared her. "That might be taking it too far."

"No, don't you see? That's exactly why you should do it. You need this type of connection with him. If it gives you a sense of déjà vu, it might do that to him, too. And he'll want to get regressed."

Caught up in the moment, Beverly agreed.

Amber headed into the house to get the artist's number and call her.

When she returned, she said, "Yasmine is on her way. See how easily this worked out?" She turned toward Beverly and smiled. "Some things are just meant to be."

~

Beverly returned to the B-and-B and stood outside the door. She'd called ahead and told Jay that she was going to be late, but she hadn't told him why.

A bit nervous, she used her key and went inside. He was sitting on the bed, watching a sporting event on TV, only he was clean shaven. At some point while she was gone, he'd gotten rid of the David beard.

"Did you have fun?" he asked, as he climbed off the bed.

She nodded. "Amber and Kiki are both really nice."

"Most people wouldn't describe Amber as nice, but I get what you mean." He made a perplexed expression. "What's all over your hands?"

Here it comes, she thought. "A friend of Amber's mother did it. Her name is Yasmine, and she's a mehndi artist. *Mehndi* means *henna.*"

"Like what women in India wear? Let me see." He came closer to inspect the work. "It's beautiful. Was it done with a stencil?"

"No. She did it freehand with these little plastic cones, like applicators used for icing a cake." Beverly had never told Jay about the henna design Camille had worn on her wedding day, and it was obvious he had no significant knowledge of this type of body art. "There are different types of henna styles. This is Arabian. The lines in Indian mehndi are finer."

"How long will it last?"

"Not that long. Maybe five or ten days, depending on how well I care for it. If it was sealed, it would last longer." She explained, "Normally Yasmine seals her designs with a paste and wraps a bandage around the area, but I wanted you to see it right away so I asked her not to seal it. It'll darken over the next few days."

"Then it will fade?"

"Technically, henna doesn't fade. It's actually the skin exfoliating that makes it disappear."

He inspected her hands again. "It's fascinating."

Yes, she thought, but it wasn't having a déjà vu effect on him. Should she tell him that it was a bridal tradition or that his name was hidden in the pattern?

She opened her mouth to say it, but she couldn't. Because as Jay continued to study her hands, the significance of the design affected her in a way she couldn't deny.

And she finally admitted, at least to herself, that she was still in love with him.

CHAPTER FIFTEEN

After Beverly and Jay returned to L.A., they fell into a busy pattern. On this hectic morning, she would be going to her next regression session, and he would be headed to the beach for a national commercial shoot.

As Beverly put a pot of coffee on, she battled her options. Should she tell Jay that she loved him? And should she ask him how he truly felt about her?

Maybe tonight, after he got home.

Home? He didn't live here; he bounced back and forth between her apartment and the house he shared with Amber and Luke.

She glanced at her hands. The henna had darkened to a

deep, rich orange, and the spot where Jay's name was hidden was especially bright.

Not that he would know the difference.

Just then, he entered the kitchen. Fresh from the shower and casually dressed, he looked tall, tan and a tad tired.

"Coffee," he said, in a jokingly desperate voice.

"It's almost ready."

He walked over to the counter, near where she stood, and watched the hot brew drip into the carafe.

"I always get a little nervous before a shoot," he said.

"I know. But you'll do a great job."

"Pimping chewing gum with a surfboard?" He laughed, albeit lightly. "At least I don't have any lines."

"That's right. All you need to do is flash your pearly whites and your six-pack."

He lifted his T-shirt and exposed the aforementioned muscles. "They'll probably airbrush them to maximize the effect." Another light laugh. "What an ego booster that is."

"As if that matters. You know darn well you're hot."

"Same goes for you."

She tried for a bit of humor that felt all too real. "I guess that means we'd have hot babies."

"Little surfers and strippers." He made a joke, too. "Can you imagine?" A moment later, he went serious. "You can hardly blame your parents for being uncomfortable about your job. I wouldn't want a daughter of ours doing what you do." He snared her gaze. "Would you?"

She could've kicked herself for opening the door to a conversation like this. "I would encourage our daughter to do whatever makes her happy."

"Yes, but wouldn't you rather see her being happy with her clothes on?" Before she could respond, he said, "Never mind. All of this is a moot point anyway."

Why? Because they were never going to have babies? His logic made her ache in all sorts of ways, but she focused on the here and now. "It hurts that you don't respect what I do."

"It's not a matter of respect. I think you're an incredible dancer, and watching you turns me on, more than you could possibly know." He frowned. "But it twists me up inside to think of you bumping and grinding for other men. A lot of guys feel the way I do. They enjoy seductive entertainment, but they don't want their girlfriends, wives or daughters doing it."

"Even if their girlfriends, wives or daughters feel empowered by it?"

"Yes, even if. And I know how that sounds, like we're the biggest hypocrites on the planet."

"You especially. Having a ménage with your best friends."

"I know," he agreed. "But if my feelings for Amber had gone beyond friendship, I couldn't have shared her with Luke. He was having all sorts of trouble sharing her with me."

"I understand that part. I couldn't share you in an intimate situation, either. I guess that's where I'm different from Camille. But she didn't have much of a choice, not when her husband owned a harem."

"At least she figured out a way to capture his attention."

"That might have turned out badly for her."

"And it might've worked out just fine. Hopefully you'll find out today."

"Yes, hopefully."

He changed the subject. "Do you want to hook up later? I'll call you after my shoot, and you can meet me at the pier."

"Sure. That sounds nice."

"Then it's a date." He leaned forward to give her a gentle kiss, and she put her arms around him, wishing that she didn't love him, wishing that she hadn't put herself in such a painful situation. When they separated, she fought the urge to cry.

"Oh, good," he said. "The coffee is ready." He proceeded to pour two cups and handed her one.

She thanked him, and they went silent.

Then he said, "It's nice that we were able to talk about this stuff without fighting. It proves that our affair is actually working."

Yes, she thought. But what if she needed more from him? How long would it last then?

They finished their coffee, and he left the house. She soon followed, and when she arrived at her destination, she took a long, deep breath, stressing over Jay and preparing to reconnect with Camille.

~

Two days after the master had tied Afyon to his bed, he requested the presence of his wife. I proceeded to the stables that morning, where our meeting was scheduled.

Fretful, I arrived early. I sat on a bench beneath a big shady tree with a view of a nearby paddock. As I waited, I watched a group of lactating mares with their foals, grateful that the women in David's harem were not permitted to bear his young. In that respect, my husband belonged solely to me.

David was precise in his arrival, neither early nor late. He approached me with a typically regal expression. I put on my royal face, so to speak, and worried about why he had arranged this meeting. Was it to discuss his latest encounter with Afyon? Or was it to accuse me of being her? I prayed it was not the latter.

He greeted me properly. "Good morning, Camille."

I spoke in kind. "Good morning."

He stood in front of me, giving me no choice but to look up at him. He was attired in his riding gear, but I expected as much.

Then much to my surprise, he did something unexpected. He reached out and lowered my veil, exposing my hair to the sunlight.

Concerned, I held my breath. Was he examining the color,

searching for a hint of the highlights that belonged to Afyon?
Or was he allowing me to forgo the usual custom since we were
the only people in this area of the stables?

"You have luxurious hair," he said.

"Thank you." I let out my breath.

"Afyon does as well."

I sucked in my breath again. "I wondered if she was your
purpose."

"My purpose for what?"

"Requesting to speak with me."

"I tied her to my bed."

I tried to act dumbfounded. I even held a dramatic hand to
my chest. "Why would you do such a thing?"

He sat beside me, his shoulder brushing mine. "To punish
her for being so alluring."

I fussed with the collar of my modest caftan. "Your reasoning is odd, David."

"One of my guests, a boyhood friend, offered to purchase
her from me after he watched her dance. He wanted her so
badly, we clashed over it."

Although I knew all of this, I behaved otherwise. "Is tying
a slave to your bed your usual means of punishment?"

"Afyon is the first. She tries my patience like no other." He
looked straight at me. "Nonetheless, she pleasured me deliciously that night. I wonder, Camille, if you could take me as
deeply." His voice turned harsh. "I suspect that you could. But

maybe, to be sure, I should order you to your knees, right now, and test your skills."

My heart beat frantically in my chest. *"Why are you speaking to me this way? I am your wife, not your slave."*

"The likeness between you and Afyon disturbs me."

"Then speak to Baki and arrange to have her sent away." At this point, I wanted Afyon to disappear. I wanted the charade to end and for David to never know the truth. Or at least never know for sure.

"I think I should bring you and Afyon together. If I put you side by side, I believe your likeness will be less disturbing."

"No" was all I could manage to say.

"No?" He raised his eyebrows. *"This is not your choice to make."*

"I will not have you comparing me to a harem girl."

"Why, Camille?"

"Because I find it demeaning."

"And I find this game of yours tiresome."

I fought to the end, even though my ship was sinking. *"What are you talking about?"*

"Spare me your theatrics. I suspected your ruse on the day Afyon presented herself to me. I inspected her body. I molded my hands to her curves. Did you think that I had so many women that I was immune to the female form? That one feels the same as another? I mean honestly, Camille, what kind of fool would I be if I did not recognize my own wife?"

I battled the sting of tears. "I never intended to make a fool of you."

"I ordered you to watch me with Sarila and Ruby. I arranged for you to dance naked for other men. I tied you to my bed. And not once did you consider ending the charade."

"You did all of those things to test me? To see how far I would go?"

"Why else would I? You frustrated me at every turn. Looking so magical. Tasting so sweet. Dancing like a sorceress in front of my guests." He narrowed his eyes. "Can you imagine how I felt when Sheikh Hayri offered to purchase you? He did not understand why I behaved in such an irrational manner over a slave. But what was I supposed to say? That the dancer he desired was actually my wife?"

I remained silent, and he continued his tirade. "I was certain that you would refuse to entertain my guests, certain that my wife would never show herself to anyone but me."

I defended my actions. "I was only trying to seduce you into loving me, and once I captured your heart, I was going to tell you the truth."

"Love?" He nearly shouted the word. "What kind of absurdity is that? If a husband is to love his wife, it will happen on his terms. She cannot seduce him into it and certainly not by enticing other men."

I ached from the inside out. "I meant well. Truly I did."

"I could kill Baki for his part in this. And Ruby and Sarila

and the rest of the harem, too. How dare they conspire against their master?"

"The fault is mine and mine alone. I ordered Baki and the girls to help me. If you kill anyone, it should be me."

He glared at me, and I fidgeted. He looked ready to strangle me where I sat.

"I am sorry, David."

"Sorry? I will never forgive you for what you have done, and when I bed you, it will be for the sole purpose of procreation. You will never mean anything to me."

"In that regard, nothing has changed," I responded. "I never did mean anything to you. Yet all of my childhood, I dreamt of the day I would become your bride. You were my heart and soul, even then."

He glanced away, as if my words affected him. In the interim, I waited, praying that he would grant me a piece of his heart.

But he turned back with the same hardened expression. "Your behavior was not befitting a princess."

"How else was I supposed to compete with your harem?"

"I told you from the beginning, a wife cannot replace a harem."

"But I did, at least for a short time. Afyon bewitched you, even though you knew she was me."

"Yes, and I struggled with her bewitchment, with the sin she was committing."

"My only sin was in loving you, David."

He refused to indulge me. He stood up and made a silent departure, leaving me with tears in my eyes and a lump in my throat. Yet somehow, I loved him still.

Beverly met Jay at the pier, where they sipped chai tea and leaned against a rail that overlooked the water. In the background, joyous sounds blasted from a beachfront amusement park.

"I kept hoping it wasn't going to turn out like this," she said. She'd already relayed the details of her regression to him.

"I'm sorry, baby. But there isn't anything you can do about it."

She watched a wave crash onto the shore. "David was so angry, so unfair."

"I know, but you have to understand his position."

"His position?" Just as Beverly's temper flared, the wind whipped her hair. "All she did was love him."

"Camille shouldn't have danced for his guests."

"David arranged it," she argued. "It was his idea."

"Yes, but apparently he didn't believe that she would go through with it. And she shouldn't have. She should have come clean before then."

"Oh, that figures. You're blaming her and making excuses for him."

"I just get the stripping thing. I've been through it, remember?"

"Like I could ever forget. You and your hypocritical ways."

"Maybe I can't help it. Maybe I really am David. And maybe once I married you, I freaked out about you being a dancer because of what Camille did."

Suddenly she felt strong and hopeful. Suddenly everything seemed to make sense. "Then fix what you screwed up in your last life, Jay. Do something about it."

"Hey, wait a minute." He turned the tables on her. "This is your regression. Your therapy. You should be the one making amends for Camille."

"How? By quitting the club?"

"Works for me."

"Right. You and David start all of this and I'm supposed to make it right."

"David and I didn't start anything. You and Camille did."

"Are you kidding? She's the one who adapted to his lifestyle."

"That's what women were supposed to do in those days."

"What? Be slaves to their husbands? Times have changed, Jay. Couples are supposed to compromise now."

He gave her a hard stare. "You didn't compromise."

She stared right back. "Neither did you."

"Which is exactly why we're not a couple anymore."

She cursed herself for loving him. She cursed Camille for loving David, too. "I can't deal with this."

"Deal with what? Us? Come on, Bev. Don't be that way. Let's just drop it."

"I can't." Because that would be like pretending that her feelings weren't real or that David hadn't crushed Camille. "I'm going to go."

"Go where?"

"Home." She needed to be alone.

"So that's it? It's going to end the way it ended before? With you walking out on me?"

"How can I be walking out on you when we're not actually a couple?"

"Damn it. You know what I mean." He tossed his empty cup toward a trash can and missed by a mile. He cursed again, then went over and picked it up, disposing of it properly.

She watched him, thinking how frustratingly beautiful he was. No other man affected her the way he did. No other man left her weak-kneed and confused.

He returned to her and said, "You're overreacting to what happened to David and Camille. Just forget about them. They've been dead and gone for centuries."

Before she did something stupid, like tell him that she

loved him, she backed away, making it clear that she was leaving.

His eyes went dark and troubled, but she didn't let him deter her. Because staying would only hurt them both, and she couldn't bear to prolong the agony any more than she already had.

CHAPTER SIXTEEN

"For cripes' sake, just call her," Luke said.

"Stay out of it," Jay shot back. A week had passed since he'd seen Beverly, and he'd been going stir crazy. This morning, he was making a huge batch of fried potatoes to go with the cheddar bacon frittata he'd just taken out of the oven. Anything to keep busy.

"You can't go around here cooking like a fiend. Amber and I are going to get fat."

Jay spooned into the potatoes and placed them next to a generous helping of the frittata. Then he slapped the plate in front of his look-alike roommate. "Amber isn't even awake yet, so just shut up and eat."

"I'll eat, but I'm not shutting up." Luke tasted the frittata.

"Damn, this is good." He motioned to the chair across from him. "Join me."

"I'm not hungry."

"Sit your ass down anyway."

"So you can hassle me about my screwed-up love life?" Jay leaned against the counter. "Thanks, but I prefer to stand."

"I seem to recall you hassling me about the same thing not too long ago."

"Yeah, and you told me to fuck off, remember?"

"True, I did." Luke crammed a forkful of potatoes in his mouth. Upon swallowing the hearty bite, he said, "But I ended up taking your advice. So now you can take mine and call her."

"And say what?"

"That you love her."

His heart banged against his chest. "Who said I—"

The other man cut him off. "Don't go into denial mode. We're both too smart for that."

Okay, so he loved her. So what? He'd loved her last time, too, and look where that had gotten him. "It won't make a difference."

"It always makes a difference."

"Not with Bev."

"Just do it."

"She's probably still asleep. She worked last night."

"You've been keeping up with her schedule? That's a bad sign. Have you been Internet stalking her, too?"

"Knock it off."

Luke shrugged. "If you're not going to eat and it's too early call her, then go take a shower. You look like hell."

"If I look like hell, it's because I've been slaving over the food you claimed you didn't want. The meal you've been shoveling into that big trap of yours."

The chow hound grinned around a mouthful. "While you're in the shower, maybe you should rub one out. It might improve that attitude of yours."

Jay raised his middle finger in the air, but he grinned, too. He loved Luke like a brother.

A shower seemed like a good idea, considering the fact that he was still in his pajamas.

He left his roommate sitting at the table and headed to the bathroom. Once he stripped down, he thought about Beverly. Should he call her? Or would that only magnify his misery?

The water hit him like pellets, pounding his body into naked oblivion. He soaped down, but he didn't slide his hands between his legs. He preferred to feel the frustration. Punishment, he supposed, for being in love.

Later, after shaving and slapping on some cologne, he got dressed and watched the clock.

Finally, at what he considered a safe hour to call Beverly, he punched out her number, cursing Luke for planting the seed. With each ring, his pulse thumped in his ears.

"Hello?" she answered cautiously.

That alone told him that his name had showed up on her caller ID.

"It's me," he said anyway.

"I know."

What a conversation. He struggled for something to say and came up with, "I was just wondering how you were doing."

"I'm okay. How are you?"

"All right." He exhaled a sharp breath. "I miss you, though."

Her voice cracked a little. "Me, too."

He fought the distance of the phone. He wanted to see her in person. "Maybe I can come over and hang out for a while."

"Sex won't solve anything, Jay."

"I wasn't proposing a quickie."

"Weren't you?"

"No." Something long and lingering sounded good to him, but he wasn't about to admit it. "I'll bring you some leftovers. I made frittata and fried potatoes. Enough for an army."

"I haven't eaten yet."

"Then let me come over and feed you." He glanced at the

clock he'd been watching. By now it was brunch time. "I haven't eaten yet, either."

"Okay," she said.

"Then I'll be over soon." The last time he'd brought her food—ice-cream sundae fixings—he'd eaten it off of her body, but he knew better than to mention it.

They hung up, and he returned to the kitchen. Luke was gone and the leftovers were in the fridge. Jay repacked it, leaving some for Amber and taking the rest with him.

As he arrived at Beverly's apartment, he asked himself if he should tell her that he loved her, just for the sake of saying it.

He knocked, and she opened the door. After that, they stared at each other. She looked as beautiful as always, with her long blond hair and golden tan.

He wished that she wasn't Malibu, that she wasn't a California-stripping bride. Or any kind of stripper, for that matter. But his wish wasn't her command. David and Camille aside, Jay wasn't her master.

"Come in," she said, ending the staring jag.

He entered the apartment. "Thanks." He held up the bag with their meal. "Ready to eat?"

She nodded.

Rather than engage in small talk and make things more awkward than they already were, he made a beeline for the kitchen, intending to reheat the leftovers.

Beverly reached for some plates, and he noticed that the henna she'd gotten on her hands was gone.

She followed the direction of his gaze and said, "I probably shouldn't tell you this, but I guess it doesn't matter now. It was a bridal design, and your name was hidden in it." She quickly added, "David's name had been hidden in the design Camille wore on her wedding day, so Amber thought I should have the artist hide your name in mine. But like I said, it doesn't matter now."

It mattered to him. "Where was my name? Show me?"

"Here." She gestured to a spot where nothing remained.

He ran his thumb over her skin, wishing his name was still there, yet at the same time wishing that he didn't love her. Proof, he thought, of how mixed up he was.

When she snatched her hand away, he realized how deeply his touch affected her.

Did she love him, too?

He couldn't bear to ask nor did he intend to admit how he felt. Being in love hadn't saved their marriage so why would it save them now?

Regardless, they were staring at each other again, locked in the kind of emotion that turned the lining of his stomach inside out. He wanted to kiss her so badly, he cursed the day they were both reborn. By now, he couldn't imagine not being David.

"Do you think this is their fault?" he asked.

She didn't question who he was referring to; she obviously knew. "Our lives are our own, Jay."

He nodded and turned away to tend to the leftovers.

She spoke again. "I have a regression appointment later."

He spun back around. "Later when? Today?"

"Yes. In a few hours. But I'm not expecting a happily-ever-after."

At this stage, neither was he, not if history was repeating itself. "I want to go with you."

"Why?"

Yes, why? "Because I'm as wrapped up in their bullshit as you are."

She frowned. "Bullshit?"

"Love, lust, whatever." He couldn't describe it, not in a way that made sense. "Besides, if I don't go with you, I'll be calling you to hear the outcome anyway."

Beverly tugged at the ends of her hair, twisting a strand around her finger. Anxiety, he thought. He understood. He wasn't faring much better. A gust of air was trapped in his lungs.

She said, "You can't go inside the session with me. You'll have to stay in the waiting room."

He released his breath. "That's fine."

Without discussing it further, they focused on their meal. He suggested eating on her balcony because staying inside seemed too intimate.

Afterward, she got ready for her appointment and when the time came, they took separate cars. It was better that way, he supposed. Less togetherness.

But being alone in his car didn't help. Jay maneuvered his way through traffic, nervous as hell.

The office was located in a professional building. He'd imagined a little room above a New Age shop or something along those lines.

He met Beverly out front and they took the elevator to the third floor and entered a suite at the end of the hall.

There was no receptionist. In fact, there was no one in the front office except them. They sat side-by-side on a sofa, the awkwardness from earlier gaining momentum.

Soon the therapist appeared from an office in the back. She was an average-looking woman, mid-forties, with light brown hair and plastic-framed glasses.

Beverly introduced her to Jay. He already knew that her name was Mary Beck. He'd seen it printed on the suite door.

He stood up to shake her hand and recalled that she was a student of Beverly's. It was tough to picture her taking strip-tease lessons. Then again, the point of the class was to teach women to explore their sensuality and attain the confidence to express it.

"It's nice to meet you," she said.

"You, too." He wondered if she was learning to be the

sexy-librarian type, flinging off those plain-Jane glasses for her husband or whoever.

Mary turned to his ex. "Ready?"

Beverly said, "Yes," and they went off to do their thing.

Jay fidgeted for a few minutes, then removed his phone from his pocket and went online.

A short time later, Beverly and Mary reemerged.

"What's going on?" he asked. He knew it hadn't been long enough for a full session.

"I wasn't able to regress," Beverly responded. "There was just nothing there."

Mary said, "We're going to try again next week."

Shit, Jay thought. "Should I leave? Is it because I'm here?"

"It could be a number of things," Mary told him. "But whatever the cause, she's just not open to hypnosis at the moment."

"Maybe I should try it," he heard himself say.

Beverly all but gaped at him. "Seriously?"

"Why not?" He was desperate for something, anything, that would give him a bit of closure, even if it was of the unhappily-ever-after kind. He turned to Mary. "Is it possible for me to take Bev's time slot?"

"You want to do it now?" the therapist asked.

"Yes," he responded. Right now. Before he lost his nerve.

Mary agreed to take him, and while he filled out the necessary forms, he glanced at his ex. She looked as anxious as he felt. She would be waiting to see what his session unveiled, if anything.

A few minutes later, the therapist escorted him to her private office, a room decorated in soothing colors and attractive furniture.

"Have a seat." Mary gestured to an overstuffed chair.

He'd been expecting a couch. But he supposed that was a cliché. He sat down. The chair was big and comfortable, but he tensed just the same.

She took a similar chair, reassuring him that they had plenty of time. The slot after Bev's appointment was free, too.

Soon he found himself relaxing. Her voice was as soothing as the color of the walls.

When the actual hypnosis began, he went dreamlike, yet completely aware, as if his conscious and subconscious minds were merging as one.

"Tell me your name," Mary said.

Jay, he thought. But he said, "David."

"David who?"

"Prince David Abir Rou Veli." Jay realized that he'd said "Prince" in another language.

"I need you to speak English," she told him.

David didn't understand English nor did he speak it, yet her request made sense. Because of me, Jay thought.

"David?" she said.

"Yes?" This time, he replied in English.

"How old are you?"

"Ten," he told her.

"I thought you were a grown man."

"Someday I will be." Jay saw David in his mind. He was a dark-haired boy, dressed in loose-fitting clothing and sitting in a spacious room with archways and mosaic floors. "My bride has already been chosen."

"Is she a princess?"

"Yes, from another land."

"Have you met her?"

"No."

"Do you want to meet her?"

"Not until it is time." He wanted to be big and strong when he saw her.

"Tell me more about what your life is going to be like when you're older."

"I will have a harem, like my father before me, and his father before him." He knew that when he came of his age, his parents would purchase his first girl.

"I think you should grow up quickly."

"Why?" he asked her.

"Because I want to speak to the David who is married to the princess. The David who already has a harem."

Just like that, the image in Jay's mind changed. He was no longer a boy. He was a tall, leanly muscled man with a close-cropped beard, standing outside the harem courtyard.

"Are you married now?" she asked.

He frowned. "Yes, but my wife betrayed me."

"How?"

He explained what she had done, emphasizing the provocative manner in which she had danced for his guests. "It has been a week since I confronted her about it. I have not seen her since."

"Are you still angry with her?"

"Yes." Jay went deeper into David's mind, deeper into his emotions. "She is with the girls from my harem, taking refuge in their company."

He walked forward, and the setting became stronger, more colorful. Jay could feel the ground beneath his feet. He could even feel David's heart beating.

He continued on his way, taking the path to the buildings. A man in the distance spotted him and rushed forward. Jay knew instantly it was Baki.

"Your Highness. If you would have summoned me, I would have prepared the girls for your esteemed presence."

"I seek my wife," David said.

"I shall bring her to you."

"I prefer to approach her myself. Where is she?"

"In Sarila's room. Ruby is there, as well. Are you certain you do not want me to—"

"Warn them that I am here?" David interrupted, annoyed

that Baki had bonded with Camille. "I think the element of surprise will be far more interesting."

"Yes, Your Highness." The eunuch was in no position to disagree.

David cut across the courtyard and entered the women's quarters, taking Jay right along with him.

CHAPTER SEVENTEEN

The halls were quiet, but David expected as much. The girls often napped at this time of day, lounging to combat the heat.

Would Camille be napping? Sharing a bed with Sarila and Ruby? The thought both annoyed and aroused him. All he had done for the past week, day and night, was long for Camille.

He pushed open Sarila's door. They were, indeed, asleep. A beautiful trio, with their shapely bodies sparsely covered and their limbs akimbo. Camille was in the middle, the other two pressed softly against her.

He imagined removing his clothes and crawling into bed with them. But he made a deliberate noise instead, tapping his feet to the floor.

Ruby cracked open her eyes, and when she caught sight of him, she shot up like an arrow, her red hair flying about her shoulders.

Swiftly, she roused the other two.

Sarila and Camille came instantly awake, and Camille stared at him as if he were a figment of her imagination. But he assured her that he was quite real.

He said to the slaves, "Prepare my wife for my bedchamber. Clothe her in a costume Afyon would wear. But do not tint her hair or create a mask for her eyes."

"Yes, Master," they responded in unison.

To Camille, he said, "Be prepared to dance."

"For you?" she asked.

"Yes, for me," he retorted. Who else would be her audience? "Bring a set of finger cymbals." He knew she had been taught to use them. "This will be a private performance with no musicians."

Without another word, he turned and left, and in spite of his strong, straight posture, his nerves jangled.

Alone with his thoughts, he spewed a string of forbidden curses. He detested feeling this way.

David had never feared anything. Yet here he was, afraid of falling in love with his wife.

He returned to his apartment and waited impatiently. He should have warned Ruby and Sarila to make haste with Camille's grooming.

Finally, a knock sounded on his bedchamber door. He opened it and saw Camille with Baki as her escort.

The eunuch immediately took his leave. David gestured for Camille to enter, and she stepped inside.

Attired in a glittering costume that fit looser than he would have preferred, he puzzled over her intent. He knew she was not concealing the swell of a child. She had yet to conceive.

Regardless, she looked the way he imagined an angel might look, radiating long, lean grace. Her thick brown hair, decorated with tiny strands of pearls, cascaded in sleek waves, and her elegantly lined eyes enhanced her beauty without masking her true self.

"I expect a stellar performance." He kept his voice devoid of emotion, when, in fact, he was feeling highly emotional.

From a small pouch, she removed a set of four cymbals, two for each hand. "Who am I to you, David? Your wife or your slave?"

He considered the validity of her question. "Today you are both."

"Then I shall behave as both, and you will not treat me badly when I am finished."

He sat on the floor amongst a grouping of pillows. "On the contrary, Camille, I will do as I see fit."

She looked him straight in the eye. "Then so will I."

He smiled, albeit slightly. "A battle of wills? How fascinating."

"Quite," she agreed.

Without sparring any further, he clapped his hands, signaling for her to entertain him.

And so she did.

She rolled her glorious body, creating music, beauty and the potential for sex.

Her costume flowed as she moved, billowing like wings. The pearls in her hair caught the light, creating an iridescent glow.

Once again, she reminded him of an angel. But Allah's angels did not sin. Nor did they tempt man. Yet on and on she went, tempting him, making him desperately hard.

Then, without warning, she stopped dancing and removed the cymbals. David opened his mouth to protest, but she pressed a finger to her lips, hushing him.

Curious, he waited.

She tossed the cymbals at him, where they hit his chest and fell into the space between his legs.

He lifted his eyebrows, and she shrugged. Bold and beautiful. Delicate and daring.

Slowly, seductively, she began to strip.

Captivated, he watched—hungry to ravish her. Her generously rouged nipples were as ripe as the red-fleshed fruit that grew wild on the palace grounds, but the flower painted around her navel caused his mouth to water. It appeared to be made of pastry frosting, with a leafy stem, also made of frosting, working its way to her vulva.

How cleverly she had hidden it beneath her costume, keeping the loose fabric from destroying the design.

Completely naked, she leaned forward to retrieve the cymbals and "accidentally" bumped his cock.

Every ounce of air rushed out of his lungs.

Camille smiled, and he fought for self-control. He could smell the sugary treat on her skin.

She picked up the cymbals and put them back on. Resuming her performance, she teased him with the flower.

David longed to taste it, but she kept moving out of reach, dancing around him in an untouchable circle.

Finally, he managed to grab hold of her. Grasping her hips, he pulled her toward his mouth and trailed a wet path from her navel to her vulva. He licked and licked, eating the frosting from her skin.

Eager for more, he parted her slick folds and tasted her there, too. She moaned softly and rocked against his tongue. In a sense, she was still dancing. He could hear the cymbals chiming.

She seemed desperate to orgasm, and that aroused him beyond compare. He pleasured her vigorously, allowing her juices to flow into his mouth.

When it happened, when she spun into completion, her entire body rippled, deepening his desire.

Afterward, he freed his erection, and she slid onto his lap. Automatically, she impaled herself, taking him inside. She rode him, up and down, milking him, making him crazy for her.

Trapped in a game he could no longer control, he pushed her down and climbed on top. He thrust hard and deep, and as she looked into his eyes, he battled the vicious beating of his heart.

She wrapped her arms around him, and the cymbals attached to her fingers dug into his back.

Marking him. Branding him.

He thrust harder, and she kept his pace, absorbing the powerful rhythm. Rolling over the floor, they clawed and kissed and bit lustfully at each other's lips.

He pinned her down and spilled into her. She climaxed, too, and he wondered if their souls were as deeply connected as their bodies.

Before his thoughts betrayed him further, he pulled out and stood up, leaving her panting on the floor.

David walked away and began preparing a bath for himself. She soon followed. He could feel her behind him.

He spun around. "What do you want?"

"Why did you have me dance privately for you? What was the purpose of this?"

"The purpose," he snapped, "was to clear my mind."

"Of what?"

"The constant memory of you dancing for my guests, of me clashing with Hayri over you."

"I wish it did not plague you so."

And he wished that she had not stolen into his heart, tearing him up inside. "Well, it does."

She gathered her strewn clothing. "I will summon Baki to fetch me."

Unable to let her go, he lashed out. "You are not leaving."

She glared at him. "Yes, I am."

Desperate to keep her, he lowered his defenses. She had warned him not to treat her badly. "Stay, Camille. A wife should bathe with her husband."

"Is this your way of forgiving me?"

"No," he responded honestly. "But it is my way of admitting how painfully I love you."

She caught her breath. "You love me? Oh, David. Truly?"

"Yes." He reached for her. "Truly."

She moved forward, and he took her in his arms and held her as close as an unforgiving man possibly could.

❧

Jay and Beverly stood on the street corner outside of the therapist's office, discussing his session. Or awkwardly stumbling through it, he supposed.

"He actually told her that he loved her?" she asked.

"Yes." David had done what Jay had been unable to do.

"But he didn't forgive her?"

"No, he didn't." In that regard, he and David remained the same. Jay couldn't let Beverly off the hook, either. He couldn't come to terms with her dancing.

"I wonder what will happen in your next session."

Feeling trapped within himself, he crossed his arms. "I'm not doing this again."

"Why not?"

"Because it's enough, Bev." And it was all he could handle. Emotionally, he was spent.

"Don't you want to know if he ever forgave her?"

"It doesn't matter."

"It does to me."

She crossed her arms, too, and he realized how guarded they looked, standing on a city sidewalk with cars and buses rolling by.

He said, "If it matters to you, then you should continue your sessions."

"I plan to. But you're part of it, too."

"Part of what? Their problems? If everything turned out hunky-dory, we wouldn't be rehashing some of the same issues in this life."

She tightened the hold on herself. "You're still so much like him."

"Stubborn?" He managed a pained smile. "You're still like her, too."

"A woman who likes to dance naked?" She didn't return his smile. "There's nothing left for us to do, is there?"

He knew she meant about their relationship. "We got divorced for a reason."

"I guess this is where we part ways for good."

"So it seems." He wanted to reach out and hold her, the way David had held Camille, but he knew it would only intensify the ache.

Beverly's breath hitched. "At least we got the chance to learn about who we used to be and what brought us to this point."

He struggled to lighten the mood. "Yeah, and we got to mess around for a little while."

She finally smiled. "Now we know where we got our food fetish from, too."

"David licking icing from Camille's body? That was cool. What we did was cool, too." He thought about the Sunday sundae and every other amazing moment with her. "It's going to be tough to replace you, Bev."

"You, too." Her eyes turned watery. "I suppose that means we'll probably have to do this again in another life."

"Like the screwed-up soul mates or twin flames that we are?" He brought his hand to her cheek. "Don't cry."

She tried to blink away the evidence. "I'm not."

He lowered his hand. "You take care, okay?"

She kept blinking. "Our relationship is ending friendlier this time."

"I guess that proves we've grown a little." But it didn't hurt any less. He had an ache the size of David's temper coiled like a snake in his chest.

"Bye, Jay."

"Bye."

She didn't extend her arms for a hug and neither did he. They turned in opposite directions and walked toward their cars.

He fought the urge to glance back. Hell, he fought the urge to call her name and tell her he couldn't live without her. But that wasn't the issue. Living *with* her was the problem. If he couldn't bring himself to accept her job, if he couldn't embrace that side of her, they would always end up back at square one.

So he continued walking, leaving the woman he loved and hating himself for it.

~

Beverly remained in her car until Jay drove past. Then she got out and returned to Mary's office with tears flooding her eyes.

She sat in the reception area until Mary came out.

The other woman started. "What happened? What's wrong?"

"I want to try the regression again."

"Oh, honey. You're too emotional for this. You already had trouble earlier." Mary sat beside her. "You have an appointment for next week. We'll do it then, okay?"

"I can't wait that long. Please, can't you take me today? I promise to calm down, and I'll stay here until your other appointments are over."

The therapist sighed. "What do you think this is going to accomplish?"

"I need to be with Camille."

"With Camille or with David?"

"Both."

"You can't use David as a substitute for Jay."

"If I am, I'm not doing it on purpose." Beverly rubbed her hands across her tear-smudged face. "We broke up again. Shouldn't it be getting easier instead of harder? Shouldn't I be used to it by now?"

Mary patted her knee. "I'm sorry it turned out this way."

"Please, can we try another session today? Maybe if you take me further into David and Camille's life, maybe it will help me cope."

"It's doubtful that David ever forgave Camille."

"That's what Jay said. But I need to know for sure."

"Okay. I can do the session after lunch. But however it turns out, I think this should be your last regression."

"So I can move on with my own life? With or without Jay?"

"Yes," Mary said. "With or without him."

~

The harem garden bustled with activity, but it always did when the children were there.

Johara, my two-year-old daughter, toddled about with

leaves in her hands, handing them out as gifts. She was quite the jewel, living up to the meaning of her Neylanic name.

Adem, my four-year-old son, was also engaged in the flora. He gathered lemons and placed them in a basket. But when the mood struck, he would toss them, too. In his company were three beautiful women, catering to his every whim and chasing after the lemons.

"Someday he will be a much-loved master," Sarila said.

I nodded. He was very much like his father. But even so, I was uncertain about how I felt about Adem acquiring slaves.

"Would either of you leave the palace if you could?" I asked Sarila and Ruby. "Would you want to be free?"

"Not me," Sarila responded. "This is my home."

"I am happy here, too," Ruby said.

I glanced about, certain that there were other girls who would rather have husbands and children of their own instead of sharing mine with me.

But regardless, we were a family, and I loved David's other women, just as they loved me. They had become my sisters in every way.

Baki entered the garden with a scowl on his face, and I waited for him to approach me, concerned about his expression.

"What is wrong?" I asked.

"The prince is in one of his moods."

"That must mean Sheikh Hayri has been to the palace."

Whenever he visited, my husband was reminded of the day I had danced for his guests. "Did Hayri inquire about Afyon?"

"He always does. He still wants her for his harem."

I sighed. "After all these years, why has he not forgotten her? He only saw her that one time."

"I think it is her mystery that keeps him intrigued. It could be a bit of rivalry, too. The sheikh has always coveted the prince's most prized possessions, even when they were boys."

Would Hayri be even more intrigued if he knew that Afyon was actually David's wife? "That is foolishness."

"Maybe so, but His Highness requested your presence in his bedchamber."

"Now? At this early hour?"

Baki nodded and stood off to the side, waiting to escort me. While he waited, Johara toddled up to him and held out a leaf. He accepted the gift with pride. Baki was extremely fond of my daughter.

I smiled at my little girl, then turned to admire her brother. It was such a lovely day, and I did not want to face David's foul mood. But when he called, it was my duty to go to him.

As Baki walked me to David's bedchamber, I reminded myself that the prince was a remarkable man: an adoring father, an attentive husband and an affectionate master.

But once I was inside his room, he spoke in a distant tone. "Hayri was here."

"Yes, I am aware."

"He is like a brother to me. Otherwise I would refuse his visits." David's voice went tight. "But this would not be an issue if you had not tempted him with Afyon's charms."

"Please," I implored him. "When are you going to release those feelings?"

"Never. Afyon should have belonged solely to me."

"She did belong to you. She still does. I created her for you."

"That does not change how Hayri feels about her."

"Then what is the point of you summoning me? What is it I am supposed to do?"

Frustrated, he pulled me tight against him. "Make love with me. You and Afyon."

I did not smile, not while he was frowning. But I was pleased by his request. He needed his wife, but he needed his favorite harem girl, too.

He began removing my clothes and putting his possessive hands all over me.

As we tumbled into bed, as he kissed me with unbridled passion, I quavered from his touch. No matter his temper, no matter his faults, his love for me ran deep.

But even so, I would always long for his forgiveness.

~

As clouds of perfume mingled with the scent of hairspray, the snap of locker doors collided with the sometimes friendly and sometimes bitchy chatter of half-naked females.

The familiarity should have put Beverly at ease. But she was having an anxiety-ridden night, and gazing at herself in a wedding dress wasn't helping.

"I wonder if I should change my character," she said to Delilah who sat next to her at the mirrors.

"To what?" the Roman goddess asked.

"I don't know. Maybe a harem girl."

The other woman turned to eyeball her. "You don't look like a harem girl. Besides, Karma already has that character."

"Masters had more than one girl, so why can't the club have more than one? And how do you know what a harem girl is supposed to look like?"

"Everyone knows they have dark hair, silly."

Beverly could've argued that David's girls had been captives from all over the globe: blondes, brunettes and redheads. But Delilah didn't know about the prince or his struggle over his dancing-girl wife.

The same struggle Jay was having.

Two days had passed since they'd said that painful goodbye. Two days that felt like an eternity. All she wanted to do was curl up and cry.

"You know what else?" Delilah said, interrupting Beverly's I-miss-him-so-badly thoughts. "Malibu would be a weird stage name for a harem girl."

"So I can change it."

The Roman goddess packed on a glob of mascara. "To what?"

Afyon, she thought. "I don't know. I should probably just forget it. I should probably just forget everything and go home."

"Why? Are you sick?"

Yes. Sick at heart. "Dancing here doesn't feel the same anymore."

"It's a burnout business."

"I know." But it was more than that. It was what she'd lost to be here: the man she loved, a marriage that should have thrived.

Was she using her job as an excuse to rebel against Jay and her family and everyone else who disapproved? Or was dancing at the club truly her empowerment?

Delilah stood up and adjusted her itty-bitty toga. "You look confused."

"I am. Will you do some extra sets? Will you take my place on stage tonight? I need some time to think."

"Sure. I could use the extra money." The goddess gave her costume another tug. "But maybe I should peek through the curtain to see what's going on out there."

Beverly smiled. Delilah was a quirky soul. "You always do that."

"It helps me relax." The brunette dashed over to the curtain and peeled it back a smidgen.

"See anything interesting?"

"You'll probably think so." Delilah made a face. "Remember that guy who looks like your ex or is your ex or whatever?"

Oh, God. "Is he out there?"

"Yes."

"Are you sure it's him?"

"Uh-huh."

Beverly approached the curtain, needing to check for herself. She peeked out and scanned the busy club. Jay was at the tip rail.

"I told you," Delilah said, cramming her head next to Beverly's. "He's probably waiting for you to dance. Do you want to take your sets back?"

"You keep them. I'm not going on stage." She couldn't go out there and perform, not with the way her heart was blasting inside her chest.

"Do you want me to tell him that you're going home?"

"No. I'll talk to him." There was no way she could leave without knowing what was on his mind. "I never expected to see him again, let alone see him here."

"He was here before."

"That was different." She felt certain that Jay hadn't returned to resume their affair. Or start a new one. Or . . .

Or what? Tell her that he'd changed his mind about being married to a stripper? She was more confused than ever.

Beverly inhaled a cleansing breath or as cleansing as the heavily scented air would allow.

She exited the dressing room and stepped onto the main floor. Jay didn't notice her because he was facing the other direction.

Without giving herself too much time to think, she came up behind him and put her hand on his shoulder.

He turned, and their gazes locked.

"I can't believe you're here," she said.

"I couldn't stay away" was his reply. "I haven't been able to eat or sleep. I haven't even been able to cook. You know it's bad when I can't cook." He cleared his throat. "I love you, Bev."

Heaven on earth. She pitched forward. "I love you, too."

"I want to make it work," he said. "I want you in my life. And if that means learning to accept your job, then that's what I'm willing to do."

She wanted so badly to hear those words, to live that dream, but now that it was happening, reality quickly closed in on her. "You can't just make your jealousy go away."

"No, but I can get counseling this time. I owe that to you, to us, to myself."

Her eyes watered. Good tears. Happy tears. "You know what's funny? I was debating if I should quit working here. I was going to go home and think about it."

He reacted like a man in love. "Whatever you decide, I'll support your decision. I just can't bear to lose you again."

She touched his face, putting her hand against his jaw. "Camille would be proud of you, Jay."

"And David would be rolling over in his archaic grave."

"Yes, such a spoiled boy, such a temper." She told him about her final regression. "But I'm going to miss him and Camille. I'll miss the harem, too."

"Me, too. When I was inside his head and I walked into the harem, I felt a rush of excitement."

From being in a place inhabited by beautiful women, she thought. "Do you want another taste of that?"

"What do you mean?"

"The dressing room." She gestured to the back of the club. "Come on, I'll take you."

"You're not allowed to bring guys back there."

"The other girls will cover for me. Some of them have done it before. And the bouncer at the door won't give me any trouble. I'm one of his favorites."

"Gee, that's comforting. With my luck, he's probably Sheikh Hayri's incarnate."

She laughed. "He likes me because I slip him extra tips."

Jay laughed, too, and upon entering the dressing room, he was bombarded with catcalls and flirtatious smiles. A few dancers even tried to pinch his butt, but Beverly shooed them away.

"Are you getting that rush?" she asked.

He nodded, and she got the wild urge to fuck him sense-less. Right then and there.

She took him past the mirrors, where a hodgepodge of roll-ing racks crammed with costumes shielded them from view.

"Wait here," she told him.

Beverly returned to the mirrors and asked if anyone had a rubber. In this group, she figured that somebody would be equipped.

An outspoken redhead dressed like a pole sliding, hose-busting firefighter was the first to volunteer. "I've got what you need, sugar."

The fire girl dug around in her purse, and soon Beverly took possession of the condom. By now all of the other danc-ers knew what was about to happen, but she didn't care.

She wound her way through the racks to get to Jay. She held up the protection, then tucked it into his front pocket. He grabbed her, and they groped like mindless teenagers.

"This is hot," he said.

"I thought you might like the idea."

She removed her panties, and he unzipped his pants and pushed them past his hips. He was already half hard. Beverly reached down to stroke him, giving him a full-blown erection. She rubbed the tip, over and over, making his cock jerk in her hand. She played with his balls, too, separating the tender sacs until they grew tight.

Sweet, sexy foreplay.

He put his hands under her naughty little wedding costume and fingered her until she was wet. But that wasn't enough for him. He dropped to his knees and flicked his tongue over her clit.

Beverly bunched up her dress so she could watch him torture her. He was being deliberately gentle, driving her wild with every move he made.

While he tasted her cream, he ran his hands up and down her legs, stroking her stockings and toying with her garter belt.

Beverly rocked her hips and bucked against his face. In the throes of a shudder, she came, warm and slick—all over his mouth.

Jay stood up and tore into the protection. When he pressed her against the wall, she moaned her excitement.

He thrust deep, then crushed her mouth with his, kissing her with hunger and need. She clutched his ass and pulled him closer.

Going at it in the back room of where she worked created a heart-thrilling frenzy. She could hear music from the stage and conversations from the women in the dressing room. But all that mattered was him.

The rhythm of Jay.

He filled her with passion, with heat, with lust. While they fucked, he undid the front of her dress, tugging until her breasts popped out.

There went his mouth. Sucking on a nipple. She tipped her head back, tapping the wall. Caught between melting and moaning, she held on for dear life—this one and the one they'd lived before.

He sucked the other nipple, and she knew she was going to come. But so was he. She could feel the pressure building in his loins. Love and sex and the man connected to her soul.

"Promise you'll marry me again," he rasped against her ear.

"I will," she responded, still clutching his ass. Together they were about to burst.

His body jerked first, his glutes tensing beneath her hands. Beverly went off a second later, her libido orbiting the earth and shattering into a zillion pieces.

In the breathtaking aftermath, he pressed his forehead to hers, and she wrapped her arms around him.

"A big church wedding," he said, continuing the marriage talk. "With you carrying a pink bouquet. The roses I owe you."

She smiled against his cheek. "Is that your way of trying to make a proper girl out of me?"

He laughed, and she suspected that he was envisioning how they looked this very instant, with a lace dress bunched to her hips and his pants pulled down to the crack of his butt.

"I'm just trying to keep you," he said, going serious.

She held him tighter. "Until the end of time?"

"Totally."

"Then I'm yours." She closed her eyes and let the feeling sweep her away. He was still inside her.

And forever didn't get any better than that.